A Loving Wife

VIOLET WEINGARTEN

A Loving Wife

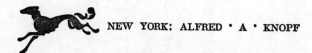 NEW YORK: ALFRED · A · KNOPF

FOR VIC

A Loving Wife

CHAPTER 1

  Molly would have preferred a day flight (when she was with Mike, they always tried to save time by flying at night) because streaking through the trackless dark gave her a sense of circling from nowhere to nowhere. "It's like being on a Flying Dutchman," she once explained to him, vainly. "It's not that I'm frightened, and it isn't claustrophobia. It's more like taking ether. I get the feeling everything is going to go on forever."

  It was different flying by day. There was the land or sea below, ordinary, recognizable, reassuring. If they took off in fog or rain, there was the sudden blinding blue of the sky above the cloud barrier, a cliché—"even if you can't see it, the sun is always shining somewhere" —Land of Cockaigne, still she caught her breath with delight each time she saw it.

But a day flight to Rome proved impractical. With the six-hour difference in time, it would get her to her hotel around two o'clock in the morning—an odd hour, for a woman alone.

So she was on a night flight after all. The plane left New York late, after waiting patiently in the lowering June twilight for nearly an hour, lined up on the runway nose to tail with other Europe-bound jets, like a great lumbering elephant at a water hole. When its turn finally came, it plodded to the take-off line, engines roaring, and then, at the last second, a voice had snapped "Abort, Number Two . . ." before the intercom cut off, the roaring ceased, the plane swerved to the right, and the next one glided into the vacated place.

After another long wait, they took off in the same plane.

"It was nothing," the stewardess shrugged, passing out limp, cold sandwiches, "just to make sure." With her black apron and scuffed ballet shoes, she looked like Sophia Loren dispensing pizzas in a Naples slum.

Molly was sure it was nothing, too. And if it was, what difference did it make now? Even so, she had kept an eye on Number Two engine this time, all the way across the Atlantic. She never did sleep on a plane. She could never sleep anywhere except in bed, curled under the cover of night. Lately she had not even been sleeping there. She had been walking around so groggy for lack of sleep that she felt drugged. As she did now. It had been a long nine hours. But the seat-belt light just went on. In a few minutes the NO SMOKING sign would flash, and they would be in Rome. The plane had already made a stop at Orly, landing and taking off without incident, so apparently Number Two engine had survived the ocean crossing, but she still fished around in her mind for a properly fatalistic image to sustain her through the final landing—a cosmic map showing the earth as a flyspeck among the stars, Nirvana, the hordes of people sleeping on the streets of Calcutta, the possibility that she had cancer unbeknown to herself and was going to die anyhow.

Not that Molly was afraid of flying. Not in the least. After all, she wasn't even needed as a mother any more, now that David was grown up, and sleeping with a girl besides. But she did not believe in tempting fate. Once on a plane, she resolutely, if temporarily, cut all the cords binding her to life. She never made a list of anything she had to do, or wrote a letter that required mailing, or did anything else that indicated in any way that she ever expected to touch earth again.

Now she straightened the back of her seat, moved the small pillow behind her head to her lap (she had read somewhere that pilots always did this upon landing when they were flying as passengers), snapped her seat buckle shut. Instantly she had a flash of Robert stalking about the dining room of his Park Avenue apartment, coffee cup in one hand and the *Times*, folded, in the other. He never could sit still. (Or would he be in the country? It would be Saturday in New York, too, by the time the news reached them.) He

11

would be glancing casually at the list of "DEAD IN ROME
CRASH" to see if he recognized any of the names. Then
his eye would light on "GILBERT, Molly: New York
City." He didn't even know she had left. What would
he do? What does a lover do in such circumstances?
Drop the cup? Say "My God" to his wife before he
catches himself? He would have to say something.
Jane would be puzzled if he didn't. After all, he
did know her. He would have to have some reaction.
Then he would probably be forced to sit through some
sort of memorial service for her. He might even be
asked to deliver a eulogy on behalf of the Center. They
would have to do something in the absence of a corpse.
They couldn't just pretend she never happened. It
would be marvelously ironic. Too bad she couldn't be
there to hear him. It would be fascinating to see what
he came up with, she thought, and suddenly she
wanted him so badly her stomach turned over.

At this point the stewardess, back in her hat and chic
in navy blue, thrust a tray of Perugina hard candies at
her. Startled, she took one and unwrapped it slowly.

The persistence of childhood, Molly reflected, putting the candy in her mouth. The fantasies never
change. She had been dreaming up the same funeral
with which she used to put herself to sleep night after
night as a child. Only then it was her mother whom
she had conjured up, dissolved in tears and ridden
with remorse. Always the same, the victim masquerad-
ing as the chief mourner.

Was she really so angry at Robert that she had to kill him in a plane crash? Was that why she had worried so about his having a heart attack while they were together? Was it only wish fulfillment? Was that the reason she had lain awake night after night wondering whether she should call a doctor, and wait, or notify the hotel desk and run, her love manifest by absence, not presence?

It was not possible, she thought. Even now the idea of his dying made her feel faint. She clutched her elbows over the seat belt and rocked like an old Jew at the Mourning Wall.

Or was it Mike she was murdering? Her arms tightened even more and the buckle of the seat belt cut into her flesh. She was coming closer. If there was any projecting it was there. Mike was the one she had betrayed, the "wronged husband," therefore she was punishing him. She was erasing him, trying to wipe out what she had done. She had hurt him, and so she was furious at him. That was the usual logic too. She remembered how he had stood in the doorway the night before—or was it the night before that, by now?—and she could taste the bile in her throat. She slumped in the rigid seat.

Whom was she kidding?

Whom did she think she was kidding?

Enough of games. Enough of Freudian blocks, of repressions, suppressions, displacements, projections. The truth was flashing in front of her.

13

A LOVING WIFE

She had the right victim in the first place.

One way or another, she had been trying to kill herself for months. And she knew exactly when she had made the first attempt.

CHAPTER 2

It had been years since Molly had seen Erna Ross—Erna Anielo, that is. They were never really friends, but they had known each other for a long time, ever since Erna married Sam Ross, Mike's roommate his first year at Hopkins.

Sam was a biochemist, too, but unlike Mike, he had no interest in research—except, of course, for what he personally could get out of it. He always wanted to make money. He went to work for a pharmaceutical house right away, learned the business fast, and then went out on his own. Erna kept the books in the beginning, Molly remembered, but not for long. Sam made a few lucky guesses, and before anyone knew it he was a success. He and Erna had two pudgy children and a big house in Roslyn, and they both took up golf. They were

passionate golfers. Then, one June day, Erna brought
the children in to New York, put them on the train for
camp, walked out of Grand Central, caught a bus for
Provincetown, and never went back to Roslyn again.

Molly still didn't know what made Erna leave. It
wasn't because of Alberto. Erna didn't meet him until a
month or so before they were married, and the wedding was on New Year's Day. Molly was sure of the
date because she and Mike went to the wedding. They
had been surprised when Erna invited them, and Mike
balked at going, but Molly had insisted. "We have to,"
she had said. "The poor thing probably doesn't know
another soul. Sam was always the gregarious one." The
wedding was in the art gallery where Erna worked.
When the Gilberts got there, they could hardly make
their way in, the place was so jammed.

They saw the Anielos a couple of times after that.
They visited them at their old farmhouse in North
Salem (Alberto had his studio in the barn), and then,
a year or so later, they met them at a Guggenheim
opening. Erna had gained weight (she had learned to
bake bread, she told them), and her seal-slick black
hair was now fuzzy and streaked with gray, but she
looked serene as a Renoir in the midst of the spiraling,
Pop Art mob.

The opening must have been four or five years ago.
They had not even spoken on the telephone since then
until Erna had called Molly at the Center that fall
morning and asked if she was free for lunch. She was,
and they had agreed to meet at Longchamps.

Erna dispensed with chit-chat abruptly. "Yes, they're still living with Sam in Great Neck. You knew he married again, didn't you?"—and came to the point quickly. She needed a job. She thought Molly might have some leads for her.

"I don't want to work in a gallery," she explained. "Alberto and I are disgusted with the whole art scene these days. It's so commercial, just one big put-on, no honesty, no decency . . ." She stopped mid-sentence and smiled. "I'm sorry. Don't let me get started. I'm paranoid on the subject." What she had in mind, she said, was a job in social work, part time, perhaps, or was a degree necessary even for that? Erna had started at the New York School at the same time Molly did, but she quit after six months. She said the school's approach was too threatening, Molly remembered now, and she was afraid it might jeopardize her marriage, if she had to choose between Sam and the New York school, there was no question which came first. Ah, well.

"I don't really need to work," Erna was saying now. "We manage fine. But I thought it would take some of the pressure off Alberto if I took a temporary job. Then he wouldn't have to push to assemble enough pieces for a show. He can just follow where his daemon leads him."

She stopped to order the cold salmon, after exclaiming at the price, and leaned toward Molly. "He's creating a whole new world, you know. Every time I walk into the studio and look around, I get so excited I could burst."

Molly thought one of the new Federal projects might be a possibility, if they got funded in time. There was also a psychiatric aide training program in the Bronx, which might be convenient for commuting, if Erna wanted to drive. She was not sure how much they were paying, but the work might be exciting.

"I'm not looking for excitement," Erna told her, "just grocery money." She stared over the crowded tables for a moment and turned back to Molly. "Don't get me wrong. It's not that money means anything to us. That's immaterial. Whether we have a lot or a little, we're still rich. We're the luckiest people in the world. I'm in love with him, and he's in love with me, and it's been that way from the first moment we set eyes on each other. When Alberto walked into that gallery, I took one look and I said to myself: 'My God, what an attractive man!' and then, the next thing I thought was that I was going to marry him. I didn't care if he had a wife and four children, or not."

"Did he?" Molly had wanted to ask, but she said nothing.

"Of course I got cold feet. We spent the whole day together, but when Alberto asked me to go home with him, I asked him if he was married before I said okay. 'I want to get it straight from the beginning,' I told him. 'This is it for me. If you don't feel the same way, let's skip it.' 'But I do,' he said, and that's how it's been ever since." She smiled, and her voice was very soft. "Who would have expected anything like that to happen to me?"

Molly tried to say something but her throat was so dry she could only cough.

"Nothing else matters, does it?" Erna said.

"No," said Molly, finally. "Nothing." She took a deep breath. "I don't know how people manage to go on without it," she said in a tight voice.

"I'm sure most people do. I did, all the time I was with Sam, and what's more, I knew it."

So do I, Molly thought.

Suddenly Erna looked at her watch and pushed back her chair. "It's only two o'clock. If I rush, I can probably make the two-fifteen." She put two crumpled dollar bills on the table. "You don't mind waiting for the check, do you?" She rose. "I'm acting like an absolute idiot, I know it, but it's the first time I've been this far away from Alberto since we got married, and I can't wait to get back. I'm afraid . . ." She hesitated and, to Molly's horror, her eyes filled with tears. "If anything ever happened to him, I think I'd kill myself."

After Erna left, Molly put ten more dollars on top of the check. That ought to cover it, she thought, but even after the waiter picked up the money, she remained seated, a pillar of stone, Lot's wife daring to look homeward, until the hostess came over and stood behind her. Then, finally, Molly got up and walked out of the restaurant like a sleepwalker. She went to the intersection of Madison Avenue and Fiftieth Street and was halfway across when a taxicab screeched to a halt a few inches away from her elbow and a man's voice shouted: "Why don't you look where you're going?" She shrugged and continued to the other side, unperturbed. She walked another two blocks before it struck her that she *had* looked where she was going, very carefully, and that she had only started to cross when she was sure the taxi was coming toward her.

She hurried back to her office then. She closed the door behind her and sat at her desk, staring at the wall in front of her. It was covered with pictures. There was a framed snapshot of Mike and David playing catch. David must have been about twelve or thirteen when it was taken. Next to that picture there was a large, red and black crayoned batlike shape which had been drawn years ago by a boy at Oak Hollow, the Center's residential treatment center for emotionally disturbed children. She had put it up because it reminded her of a Baskin. She looked at the bat shape for a while and tried to figure out just how much time she had ahead of her. Thirty years? Forty? Unless they had heart attacks, people seemed to live forever.

She took out her compact and looked in the mirror. For a moment she did not recognize herself. Her mouth was two straight lines and there were black pits under her eyes. A death mask. She applied lipstick with a firm hand and filled in the shadows with powder.

"You are forty-two years old," she informed herself, "and nothing is going to be. It is."

CHAPTER 3

It would have passed, Molly was sure. She would have shivered with discontent for an afternoon or so, and then she would have reached for a sweater. She was never happy being unhappy. It would have struck her what it was Alberto Erna was so mad about, for God's sake. She herself wouldn't have been able to stand him for twenty-four hours. She would have written off their relationship as symbiotic, suffocating, doomed. Marriage could not flourish in a closed house; it needed air.

After all, Molly was an expert on marriage. Certified. She had even taken a refresher course in marital counseling when the Center decided to serve adults as well as children. "No child lives in a vacuum," Angela Goulding, the director, had told the board in her plea for greater eclecticism. "If we want to treat the whole child, we must be prepared to concern ourselves with his entire life spectrum." The board agreed, and over the last five years, the Center had become a miniature welfare state, dispensing a rainbow of services to the families of its troubled children. It sent a homemaker when a grandmother fractured a hip and provided group therapy for parents of daughters about to give birth to interracial babies. Its caseworkers spoke knowingly of "grass" and "hash," its pediatricians dispensed contraceptive pills, and its counseling service was jammed. As an adviser, Molly tended to feel that passion counted less in a marriage than compatibility. "He's a nice place to visit but are you sure you want to live there?" she would ask a client headed for a clearly unsuitable marriage. On the other hand, it was a mistake to expect perfection in marriage, as in any other human institution, she would point out. Marriage was like the weather, she would say, sometimes good, sometimes bad, every once in a while perfectly terrible, with freezing spells, drought, storm, heat wave or, worst of all, endless stretches of fog when all one could do was wait and hope for sun.

Her mood would have passed, no question about it. But before she had a chance to grope her way out of the fog, while she was sitting there at her desk, staring at the Baskin bat, Angela burst into her office (without knocking first, Molly remembered noting instantly, something very serious must have happened).

"They walked out at Oak Hollow," Angela had announced. Her chin was trembling so violently she had difficulty getting the words out. "Sandy just called. He says they're on their way over here to picket. They may even picket Ralph Low's house." Ralph Low was the president of the Center.

"Oh my," said Molly. She was shaken, too.

"How can they do it to the children?"

How can they do it to her was what Angela really meant, Molly thought. She shrugged. "Come on, Angela, after all . . . how long have they been negotiating the new contract? Four months?"

"The board's meeting here at four o'clock," said Angela, ignoring the question. "I want you to come. It's time you started learning how to work with the trustees." Angela was always dangling her job in front of Molly. It didn't mean a thing. They both knew Angela would have to be carried out of the office if anyone tried to apply the agency retirement rule to her.

"Okay." Despite herself, Molly was flattered.

Angela had been icily calm with the board. "At the moment it's just the professional staff that's out, but I don't know if the teachers will cross a picket line tomorrow," she warned. "If they stay out, too, I don't know what we'll do with the kids."

"It's a problem," Ralph Low agreed, "but I say we don't negotiate until they go back. We gave them that fifteen-per-cent across-the-board increase last year in return for the no-strike clause, and they'd better live up to it. If they're not going to abide by their agreements, what's the sense of negotiating? A contract isn't worth the paper it's written on."

"How can they do it?" old Mrs. Miller asked in a quavering voice. She was already on the board when the Center opened Oak Hollow during the Depression. Some of the curtains she had helped put up in the cottages were still there. "After the way we care for those children!"

"Now wait a minute," interrupted Robert. He slammed his hand on the board table and everyone turned to look at him. He was astonishingly good-looking, Molly thought, very tall, very dark, very tan. It was his first meeting, too, Molly found out later. He had just agreed to go on the board as treasurer, like his father and grandfather before him. "Let's get one thing straight. We don't care for the children. Those people picketing downstairs do."

"But we pay the bills," Mrs. Miller persisted. "If it wasn't for us, there wouldn't be any Oak Hollow."

"Nope," Robert told her. "Not any more. The city picks up most of the tab. It's not our money we're arguing about, it's the city's. I don't know why we don't give them what they're asking. It's still not a living wage. You know that, Ralph. Let the city ante up more."

"That's an irresponsible position," a man Molly didn't recognize put in.

"It certainly is," said Ralph Low. "We've already ab-dicated on free choice of intake, we let the city monitor our services. If we're going to hand over budget control as well, we might as well get out of business. Who needs us?"

"It's not only a question of money," Angela put in evenly. "As a matter of fact, that's not even what they're protesting downstairs. I don't know what they've been saying in negotiations, but their public position seems to be that they're fighting for the kids, not themselves. They're handing out a leaflet with a whole list of grievances—staff shortages, tasteless food, an inadequate Board of Ed curriculum, not enough minority-group counselors . . ." She consulted a slip of paper. "They're even complaining about the clothes we issue. Listen to this: 'Second-hand citizens in outdated, second-hand clothing' . . ."

They were right, Molly thought. The children's clothes were terrible. What was it the boys in Cottage Seven had gone on a rampage for last week? Hiphuggers, that was it. They wanted no part of waist-high jeans any more. She told the board about the episode—timidly.

"Bullshit," commented Ralph Low when she was finished. "If you and the rest of the ladies will excuse me. The issue is money, pure and simple."

"I'm not so sure," Robert said. "I think Mrs. Gilbert put her finger on it. The complaints are legitimate, aren't they? Maybe we're missing a bet. If we assume that everyone's main interest is the children—and that goes for all of us, staff, board, everyone—maybe we ought to have staff represented on the board. Then

25

they wouldn't have to go around handing out leaflets to get their story heard."

"You'd have the union represented on the board?" John Simon asked him, scandalized.

"Why not?"

" 'Why not?' Hell, your father wouldn't even let the union in his plant. That's why he moved south."

"Other times, other customs. I think he was wrong."

"Well," said John, "if he hadn't, you wouldn't have a nickel today."

Ralph Low suggested they leave personalities out of the discussion. Alma Miller said that anyone who went out on strike ought to be fired, and Angela told her it would be impossible to replace them—Oak Hollow was short-handed as it was. Someone accused Robert of "denigrating" the Center and he replied: "Not at all." He thought the Center was doing a "fabulous" job, else he would not have come on the board. He believed in private social agencies, Robert said. He appreciated their flexibility and freedom to experiment. "I've worked for Adolescent House, and I tell you, the red tape a public agency has to go through would make your hair stand on end. It takes two years to get a light bulb changed." And he agreed the Center should not capitulate to *all* the union's demands.

"But I don't think it's fair to expect staff to underwrite our philanthropy either," he continued. "We don't do it ourselves. Let's face it. We don't give away a dime that's not deductible."

The meeting got nowhere.

Finally Ralph Low suggested they adjourn. "We're agreed, right? No negotiations until everyone goes back to work, right? We refuse to be blackmailed. I don't mind their being sullen, but I'm not going to put up with mutiny."

Before she left the office a few minutes later, Molly put her head in at Angela's door. Now it was Angela who sat at her desk, staring at the wall, unseeing.

"What was that about?" asked Molly.

"What do you mean?" For a moment Angela was puzzled. "Oh," she said after a while. "Our new treasurer? Oedipal. You never did hear old man Singer in action, did you? He thought Goldwater was a flaming radical."

For no good reason, Molly felt let down. "Well," she said, "see you tomorrow." She wished she could think of something comforting to say to Angela, but she couldn't. She took the elevator down and then stopped short in the lobby. She could see five pickets outside, her friend Rosalind in the lead. As she hesitated, Robert stepped out of the telephone booth next to the newsstand, and seeing her, strolled over.

"Afraid to walk the gauntlet?" When he smiled, his eyes crinkled. It wasn't just his father, Molly thought gratefully. She smiled back. "I guess so. It's like Thoreau in jail. I'm afraid they'll say: 'Molly, why aren't you here?'"

"I'll protect you, Waldo," he said, putting her arm under his. "Come on."

The picket line stopped when they appeared. Rosa-

lind kissed Molly as usual—she was a warmly demon-
strative woman—and inquired after David. Joe Green
asked if they had any cigarettes, he had forgotten his,
and Robert went back to the newsstand to buy him a
pack. When they finally departed, in an aura of good
will, they walked to the corner together and when they
got there, Robert said: "Do you have time for a drink?"
Molly, considering, told him, yes, she did.

As it happened, the teachers did not walk out at Oak
Hollow. They were said to be insulted at having been
referred to as Board of Education "rejects" in the strike
leaflet. But two days later, astonishingly, some of the
cottage parents, the men and women with whom the
children actually lived, did call in sick.

Usually cottage parents loathed social workers. "The
kid craps in my closet and when I hit the ceiling, he
tells me his caseworker says he has Oedipal problems,"
a cottage father once complained to Molly. "Do you
know how I stopped him finally? I belted him." "You
showed him you cared," Molly had retorted automatically. She was right. "Shit," said the cottage father,
and they both roared.

Molly was not sorry the cottage parents had decided
to support the caseworkers, but she was a little worried
about how Barbara Jean, one of the teen-agers she was
working with, would do with Mrs. McGinnis, her house
mother, off the premises. It was less than a month since
Barbara Jean had come to Bluebird Cottage, the house
where the older girls lived—too short a time for her to
have established any real rapport with anyone. She

ought to go out and see how things were going, Molly decided.

She had checked with Angela to see what she thought, and was just walking out of her own office when her telephone rang. It was Robert. Their direct dialing system was still so new their numbers weren't listed yet. Molly wondered how he had gotten hold of hers.

"Molly?" he said. "I've got a problem, and I think you can help me. I want an honest answer, okay?"

She was wary. "Of course."

"I don't know if you've heard about it, but some of the women in the Auxiliary are getting up a group to work at Oak Hollow. Jane, my wife, got a call and I told her I didn't want her to do it. I think it's strikebreaking. Now I've been thinking about it, and I wonder. After all, there are children left alone there. Am I wrong?"

Molly could have hugged him. "No. I really think you're right. The important thing is to get it settled quickly, not prolong the confusion by having volunteers step in. I don't think any of those women would be able to handle the kids anyhow, not the way they'll act out. They understand what it's all about. The women will just get upset. Disillusioned." She paused a moment. "At least, that's how I feel now. I'll know better after I see for myself. I'm just leaving for Oak Hollow now."

"How are you going?"

"Train."

A LOVING WIFE

"I'll drive you. I'd like to see for myself, too. I'll pick you up in ten minutes. Wait at the corner."

In less than two hours, they were at Oak Hollow. The ornate wrought-iron gates were open, as usual, and the avenue of oaks planted by the stockbroker who had owned the estate originally was a double line of flame. Apparently the teachers were still coming to work, because the children all seemed to be in school. At least, there were none to be seen. Oak Hollow looked as deceptively tranquil as usual.

"It's just the way I remember it," Robert told Molly, as they drove between the oaks. "Do you know how long it's been since I was here? Must be over thirty years. My father dragged me to some kind of picnic. I guess I was ten or eleven. I remember I didn't want to go, I was supposed to go sailing with my cousin, and I was still complaining when I got here. Do you know what my father did?" He looked at Molly with a quizzical grin. "He disappeared for a while, and when he came back, he told me he had made arrangements to leave me here with the other 'bad boys.'"

"My God!" said Molly. "You poor thing. What did you say?"

"Haven't the foggiest." He parked in front of the white-porticoed administration building and as they got out, he shook his head again. "It's amazing. Nothing's changed."

"The kids have," said Molly. "They're sicker."

"Who isn't?"

She took him to the director's office, where Sandy

was holding forth on why he was more pleased than troubled at the staff walkout. "It shows a sense of self," he said. "It shows they care. It's bound to increase the kids' respect for them."

"They won't interpret it as desertion?" Robert asked.

"No," said Sandy. "You see . . ."

Molly left them and went over to Bluebird Cottage. It was nearly lunch time. Barbara Jean ought to be there soon.

To Molly's surprise, Mrs. McGinnis was in the cottage living room, fluffing pillows. It was an astonishing room, all pink and blue, with ruffled curtains, flounced slipcovers, lace antimacassars, kewpie dolls dating back to Mrs. McGinnis's girlhood, and posters of the Rolling Stones, the Supremes, and a psychedelic guru.

"I'm not here," Mrs. McGinnis said, as soon as she saw Molly. "My bursitis is killing me."

"That's a shame. Did you happen to see Barbara Jean before you collapsed?"

Mrs. McGinnis patted her on the shoulder. "Don't worry about her, Molly. She's doing fine."

"She making any friends?"

"Relax. Rome wasn't built in a day. She eats good. We've even got her using a knife and fork," Mrs. Mc-Ginnis said with a laugh.

The first time Molly had seen her, Barbara Jean was sitting on the floor with her mother and the other children eating boiled fish heads with her fingers off a spread-out sheet of newspaper. It was the cheapest thing she could buy to eat, Julia Oglethorpe told Molly.

31

There was no other food in the house. No furniture either, except for a few cots covered with plastic sheets and a television set with a red wax rose set in a beer bottle sitting on top of it. The Oglethorpes had been on welfare, but they were off it at the time because an investigator had found a man asleep on one of the cots the week before, and Barbara Jean's mother was supposed to be "divorced."

Barbara Jean was thirteen then. Some months earlier, she had been picked up by police as she huddled in the back of a parked car with four neighborhood boys. The boys belonged to the Devil Diamond gang, the police said, the car was stolen, and all five had been smoking marijuana—an accusation Barbara Jean had denied vehemently. "I never had no joint," she protested. "I can't do it. There's something wrong with me. I can't inhale, no matter how I try. I always chokes."

Barbara Jean's arrest was actually what brought Molly to Julia Oglethorpe's Avenue A flat. It was the decisive blow needed to make her family eligible for the new interagency pilot study on "the effect of multi-faceted intensive social services on the multi-problem public-assistance family." As one of the participating agencies, the Center had drawn the Oglethorpes. Molly, intrigued, decided to take on the family herself—at least for a while. All Center executives did casework, even the director. It was a Center tradition, established by Angela when she first took over. "We must keep our hands in if we expect to keep our hearts in," she used to say.

Even so, it had been a long time since Molly had been in an Oglethorpe flat. She had forgotten the smell. Was it Lillian Wald or Jane Addams who had brought the young Mrs. Jacob Riis down to the Lower East Side and told her to take a deep breath so that she would never forget what poverty smelled like? Years ago, at the very first social-work conference Molly had ever attended, she had happened to sit at a lunch table with a birdlike old lady who turned out to be Mrs. Riis herself, and Mrs. Riis had told her of that long-ago visit. "I still remember the smell," she had said. "It was just like burnt rubber." Or stale urine, Molly thought—that was the acrid smell, more likely. It did not mix well with fish heads.

The Oglethorpes had been in the special project for three years now, and although Molly had not been to see Julia Oglethorpe for nearly a year, she did not suppose they were much better off. They were in still another flat, she knew. (In her outrage, Molly had had them back on welfare inside of a week. She had them moved out of the Avenue A hovel in another, and got them a furniture allowance.) But as long as they remained on welfare, their housing was bound to be dreadful.

The only real difference was with Barbara Jean. Barbara Jean, tested, turned out to have an I.Q. of 145 and a mild psychosis. Molly went to visit her teacher and found that she had been trying desperately to get Barbara Jean admitted to a clinic for psychotherapy. "I keep sending notes to the guidance counselor," she said, "but I don't think anyone reads them. She's a remarkable child. I've never had a pupil like her." The teacher was a tall, raw-boned woman with rheumy eyes and an urgent voice. "Look at this." She fished among a pile of papers in her top drawer and extracted two sheets of closely written lined paper. "This is how she started a report I asked them to do on the Renaissance. 'The Renaissance is my thirteenth year.' Can you imagine? In this school?" Molly saw Barbara Jean every week after that. Occasionally Dr. Ziegler, the Center's head psychiatrist saw her, too. Molly got her into a special high school and conferred regularly with the guidance counselor there. Then, after three years, just when everyone agreed that Barbara Jean was finally "over the hump" and "doing fine, maybe she could even make college," Barbara Jean had had herself admitted to Bellevue with her wrists cut.

When Molly visited her, she found her propped up in bed reading *Ulysses*.

"How do you like it?" Molly herself had skipped around until she got to the last chapter.

"It's okay," said Barbara Jean. "That namesake of yours, Mrs. Gilbert, she's a cool cat."

She gave Barbara Jean the ham sandwich and carton of malted milk she had brought with her. "Why didn't you call me?"

"What's the use? There's never going to be anything for me in this world."

Oak Hollow presently had four Negro boys in residence, courtesy of another "pilot" study (this one was entitled "integration in a private nonsectarian residential treatment center"). Molly called Sandy to tell him the title of the study was being expanded slightly to include the words "of both sexes." It was unthinkable for Barbara Jean to have to go back to her mother's house. Molly brought Barbara Jean out herself as soon as she was discharged from the hospital. "Now don't forget," she said, after they had iced tea and cookies with Mrs. McGinnis, "call me if you have any problems."

But it wasn't Barbara Jean who had called her a few days later, it was Mrs. McGinnis. "She's going to run," she reported. "Do you suppose you could come out? I think the girls are giving her a hard time."

Barbara Jean had been standing at the Oak Hollow gate when Molly's taxi drove up from the station. She had a large canvas pocketbook slung over one shoulder, and Molly could see the stuffed elephant she had given her for her birthday two years before sticking out of the top.

"I'll get out here," Molly told the driver. She walked up to Barbara Jean. "Going somewhere?" she asked.

They went out the gate together, across the highway and through the bayberry bushes and beach grass to the narrow shore. Barbara Jean took off her sandals and Molly took off her shoes, and they walked in the sand as far as the public beach and then turned around and walked in the other direction, toward the dunes.

A LOVING WIFE

The September sun was warm when they started out, but by the time they turned back, a cold wind was blowing in from the ocean. The girls in Bluebird Cottage were just sitting down for supper when they walked in the door.

"You can go now, Mrs. Gilbert," Barbara Jean said. "It's okay," and then she did something that made Molly feel as if the world were suddenly washed clean. "No," she had amended, "you stay a minute." She ran upstairs and returned immediately with an object wrapped in toilet paper and thrust into a paper bag. It was an old chrome safety razor with two separate rusty blades.

Now Molly patted Mrs. McGinnis on the shoulder. "I don't think I'll wait as long as you're around. I was just a little anxious . . ."

"You should have known I'd stick around, Molly," said Mrs. McGinnis.

Robert was talking to a group of boys around the sundial so Molly waited at one side until he saw her. He started toward her just as Barbara Jean walked down the path, arm in arm with a whey-faced girl with matted hair whose name Molly did not know. "Hi, Mrs. Gilbert," Barbara Jean called out. "I was just asking about you," said Molly. "How are things going?" "Okay," said Barbara Jean. She stopped and looked at her with an unspoken plea. "I'm in kind of a hurry," she said. "Helen and me's making the salad today." "I'm in a hurry, too," said Molly. "I just wanted to say hello."

She was shaking her head and smiling when Robert came up. "Poor kid, she was so afraid I was going to break it up."

"Break what up?"

"She's never had a friend," said Molly, and then she told him about Barbara Jean.

"Sounds like my daughter," Robert commented. "Mary's been in analysis for a year now."

"Hardly."

"Not the sex, or the pot, although I'm not even so sure about that." He was irritated. "I mean what's underneath—the craziness, the brilliance. I don't think anyone knows what the hell it's all about."

You never knew what went on with people, did you, Molly thought.

"There but for the grace of God," he said soberly, and he put an arm around her shoulder. "Let's blow. I know a great place we can eat near Babylon. Sandy invited us to lunch, but that was after he took me through the main kitchen. I told him we had to get back."

The restaurant was crowded. When the headwaiter saw Robert, he had another table put up on the outside terrace.

"Lovely," said Molly, looking around.

"I like it," said Robert. "Do you know the cottage parents aren't going back until they get a raise?"

Molly was surprised. "You mean it's not just sympathy?"

He smiled at her. "Nope. John Simon called me just before I left to pick you up, and Sandy says it's true. They want eight hundred dollars a month, contract or no contract."

"That much?"

"You're as bad as Simon. He was livid, especially since they just got the four-week vacations. I told him, 'Come on, now, how much do you pay your couple out in the country?' 'About that,' he said, 'but how can you compare . . . ?' 'Well,' I told him, 'you're a difficult man, John, I admit, but even so, I guess you're easier to be around than some of the kids at Oak Hollow. And you're in Europe most of the time, too.'"

"You sound like a troublemaker to me," said Molly. "Next thing you know you'll be fired off the board."

"Not me. They have to put up with me. Love my foundation, love me. They're stuck."

Why was he telling her all this, Molly thought, but she was pleased all the same.

"I ought to stop the *enfant terrible* bit," he said. "I'm rude, arrogant, insufferable. I know it. But those people bug me. They always have. They're so pompous, so sure of themselves—" he broke off and smiled ruefully, "I guess they remind me of my old man but it's true, most of them are only in it for diversional therapy. What gives them the right . . ."

"What gives any of us the right?" interrupted Molly sadly, and suddenly she began to tell him how irrelevant she felt, how anything she could do was so meaningless in the face of the needs. "Even if we had the money, it wouldn't make any difference," she said. "We can have special projects—like the one Barbara Jean's family is in. We can give them all the services in the book, but it's still a farce. You can't casework people out of poverty. It's like pasting paper over a rotten wall. The roaches and the rats just break through. Sometimes I think we actually make things worse."

"What do you mean?"

"Well . . ." She stopped and looked at him. "I shouldn't be talking like this to you, should I?" She paused. "What I mean is, I really think a person like Julia Oglethorpe—that's Barbara Jean's mother—is worse off than she was when we started, not better. At first, it was all right. She had absolutely nothing. You can't imagine how nothing they have. Objects we take for granted just don't exist in their lives. She got some furniture, a few clothes, better food. You could almost see her standing straighter. That first Christmas she did something really marvelous. She went down to Sally Joy Brown—that's that *Daily News* charity, they all go down to Sally Joy Brown for Christmas presents. One of the presents turned out to be a cheap camera. So she made a party for the kids. It was the first one they ever had. She got them all cleaned up and got some decorations from somewhere, and then she took each child's picture, separately, and had it developed and put in a little frame. 'I want each one to know himself,' she told me. They'd never seen themselves

39

before, you see. They didn't even have a mirror in the house."

"A sense of identity," Robert said. "A relationship to the world."

"Exactly," she said, a bit startled. "It was really beautiful."

"Then you did help her."

"Just in the beginning. When it was almost a matter of life and death. An orthopedist for one of the kids, food, blankets, a place to sit. We even got them sheets. They'd never had sheets before. But it's not good for people to get hand-outs for long, not of anything, not even advice." She leaned toward him. "There's a lot of crap in social work, especially the terminology. A lot of it ridiculous. But I used to think there was one absolute about it. If you take people who have been beaten and stepped on all their lives, people who've been knocked around so much they feel absolutely helpless, if you can give them just some glimmer of hope, some answer . . ." She smiled. "It doesn't even have to be the right answer, just so long as it's some answer, something that gets them moving again. But now I'm not sure it works out that way. Not any more. Julia used to be a pretty tough woman. Now she's a whiner. She leans. She expects everything as her due. I assigned her to another caseworker finally last year. I thought maybe she had developed a symbiotic relationship with me. But she's still leaning."

"You'd be happier if she were angry?"

"I think so," said Molly. "Not hostile angry. That

bothers me, too. Some of them are so hostile, it's sick, they go off the deep end, but . . ."

"They damn well ought to be angry. In their place, I'd want to blow the whole system up. I don't think they're sick at all. I think the ones who are sick are the ones who take it."

"That's exactly what Erich Fromm says," Molly put in eagerly.

Robert nodded. "Not that I want the anger to be directed against me personally. I didn't rape anybody's mother, I don't own any slums . . ." He stopped and grinned. ". . . any more. A few years ago, we found we owned a whole blockful."

"What did you do with them?"

"Got rid of them. Urban renewal." He put up a warning hand. "Spare me, Molly. Don't ask me about relocation. It wasn't my baby."

"I bet you made a grant to the Urban League."

"Wrong," he said. "The N double-A CP. Another drink?"

She nodded.

"I don't feel guilty," he said. "Don't get me wrong. It's an unequal world, always was, always will be."

"I can't bear it," said Molly. "I can't stand having so much while other people have so little."

"Oh, I can," he said. "If everyone had as much as I do, I wouldn't enjoy what I have nearly as much."

She was shocked. "How can you say that?"

"Because it's true. And deep down, you feel that way, too. Unconsciously, your idea of affluence is rela-

41

tive. You enjoy what you have—and therefore feel guilty—because you know other people have less. If everyone had the same, you wouldn't think you had so much, and you wouldn't enjoy it."

"I don't agree with you at all," she said stubbornly.

"Well," Robert said, "in a materialistic society, people become commodities—they're judged by what they're worth, not by what they are. Isn't that so?"

"Or by what they do. How they live up to other people's expectations."

"Exactly." He seemed very pleased with her.

I like this man, Molly decided, I like him very much. He's not at all the way he seems on the surface, he's really very sensitive. "I started to tell you about Erich Fromm," she said. "The idea of anger being less sick than adjustment. I just heard him talk at a conference and he said something about that that really shook me. I think that's when I really decided social work was just . . ." She made a helpless gesture. "Useless. Not with it. He said that by paying so much attention to individuals, instead of to the conditions that made them sick, we had created a 'pathology of normalcy.' It was that phrase, 'the pathology of normalcy.'"

"It's very good," Robert said. "You conform, you suppress, and then, one day you end up exploding . . . or dead."

"Right."

"Exactly what the kids say about us, isn't it?"

"Yep," she said, thinking of David, and was suddenly shy. "We'd better go back, Robert."

They drove in companionable silence for a while. Molly looked out of the car window unseeing, drowsy with wine and so much at peace that she was smiling without knowing it. It was a lovely spring, she thought idly, the trees at the rise ahead were all yellow, rose red, and new green. Then it struck her that it wasn't spring at all, but October, and those were not young willows in the distance but maples which would soon be left without a leaf.

"Did you ever notice," she asked, "how exactly alike spring and fall look sometimes?"

"At a certain moment in April," he said, "I see it every year when we start going up to the country again."

By the time they got to Manhattan, it was nearly five o'clock. As they drove up Madison Avenue, Molly decided that she had been wrong to tell him that Jane should not go out to Oak Hollow. It was up to Jane herself to decide. There was a legitimate reason for volunteers to go out, and she told Robert so.

"I guess you're right," he said. "I shouldn't forbid her to go. I should give her my opinion. It's all so complicated, isn't it?"

Molly agreed.

He had barely stopped in front of the Center to let her out when the policeman directing traffic at the intersection blew a warning whistle at them. "It's a towaway zone," Molly said, opening the door hurriedly, but Robert put his hand on hers and kept her seated. "We'll have lunch again soon, okay? Not this week—

43

I'm tied up. Next week, Monday or Tuesday." By then, the policeman was advancing toward them. Robert gave her hand a small squeeze, and Molly jumped out of the car. "I'll call you," he said, and drove off.

When he called on Monday, Molly asked whether Jane had gone out to Oak Hollow.

"No."

"Oh, she agreed with you?"

"No, it wasn't that," Robert said. "She forgot she had a tennis lesson."

CHAPTER 4

I must be crazy, Molly thought, torn between longing and dread, as she went through the revolving door into the lobby of the Toledo Hotel.

She stepped out uncertainly and immediately decided to go right back out again, but the door was turning so fast she had to wait for it to slow down, and during the moment she was hesitating, Robert walked over to her.

He nodded at her abruptly, took her hand and closed her fingers around a key. "You go on ahead," he said.

"Is that how it's done?" she had asked.

"That's how we're doing it," he said curtly. "Go on up, Molly. I'll see you soon."

She walked rapidly toward the elevators he indicated, every eye in the lobby focused on her, a giant

45

searchlight picking out the path she was taking. The open elevator she stepped into was unattended, but it did not move when she pushed the ninth-floor button. She looked out and saw she had to wait for the starter, standing at the bank of buttons opposite. He stared at her—accusingly? salaciously? what did his expression mean?—and then, only then, did he set her free, so that the elevator doors could close. It was an unusually rapid elevator. Before she knew it, the doors were open again, and she was forced to step out of the box. She glanced down the corridor both ways; saw, with relief, that it was empty; started to her right; realized, after a while, that the numbers on the rooms were odd, not even, like the one on the key she was holding, and, frantic, turned and ran down the corridor in the other direction until finally she was standing in front of it—910. The numbers seemed etched in fire. Molly walked up to the door but when Robert arrived, minutes later, she was still standing in the corridor outside the room key in hand, laughing.

"We'd better call it off," she told him, close to hysteria. "Keys baffle me. I've never been able to sneak in anywhere in my whole life."

"Nerves," he said briskly. "Give it to me." Then he looked at her and shook his head. "Mrs. Gilbert. The efficient Mrs. Gilbert."

He inserted the key in the lock and the door slid open. He pushed her in gently. At first all she could see were chrysanthemums. They were the size of grapefruits, so many that they hid the entire dresser mirror.

"Football weekend," she said. "I feel like a fraternity queen."

"You do?" he said, astonished. "Then what are you doing here?"

Molly looked at him for a moment, puzzled, and then flushed. "Robert, that's not what I meant!"

"I know," he said gently.

"At least they're not orchids," she said foolishly. "I hate orchids," and then she turned and clung to him. She was afraid that if she let go, she would fall because the room was beginning to spin. A fragment of melody stuck in her throat, "I love him, he is here, fa, la, la, la . . ." How nonsensical to be thinking of *The Pirates of Penzance*. It was the first matinee she had ever been to. Her father had taken her when she was a little girl. Then the melody vanished abruptly and the room stopped spinning.

After a moment she could feel Robert's hand at the back of her dress and she froze. It was a horrible mistake. She had to get out of there. What had she been thinking of, to go to bed with a stranger? Anyhow she had to take a bath first; she had a neurotic compulsion about bathing. She was a damn fool. She was jealous of every other woman he had ever taken into a hotel room, she was enraged at him—and terrified.

He lifted her chin and forced her to look at him. "What's the matter?"

"I'm scared."

"So am I," he said, "terrified," and then it was all right.

A LOVING WIFE

Afterward, as she lay with her head against his bare shoulder, he reached up and touched her cheek. It was wet.

"That's what I thought. Why?"

She turned on her stomach and looked him full in the face, smiling. "Because I was so surprised, surprised by joy!"

He never ordered the same flowers twice. The next time it was roses.

"I was so afraid to take my clothes off," she confessed. "I was afraid you'd be disappointed."

He ran his hand down her thigh. "I kept thinking I had a hole in my sock."

"You know what?" she told him, overwhelmed with delight. "You did."

Another time, there were daisies. She made a turban out of a towel and tucked one into the fold.

"Tell me," she had asked, "do I look like the *Cosmopolitan* girl?"

She was standing in the bathroom doorway, another bath towel knotted over her breastbone like a sari. She had no robe, of course. You traveled light for a journey ending in a lovers' meeting in a hotel room. She would probably never be having an affair at all, Molly thought, not for the first time, if she hadn't switched to the pill last year. It was an unromantic idea, but it was true.

It was not so much a matter of spontaneity as logistics. She could not have taken her diaphragm from its usual place without inviting suspicion and, besides, it would not have been fastidious to, so to speak, share it. But if she had bought a second one, what would she have done with it? Kept it in Robert's pocket? Certainly she could not have carried it around with her. She knew exactly what would happen. The first time she and Mike were in a restaurant, she would have taken out the diaphragm box instead of her powder compact. It was foreordained. Her conscience never made a coward of her. It marched her in front of the firing squad. Her superego was the original begetter of the Freudian slip. When she forced herself to make a dutiful phone call, her fingers dialed a wrong number. She would greet unexpected, unwanted company warmly and then hear herself murmuring graciously, "I'm so SORRY you dropped in." She could not possibly have managed both an affair and a diaphragm.

Besides, false alarm or no false alarm, the pill was statistically safer. It wasn't the pill that had just made her so late, it was guilt. No question about it. Strange, wasn't it? And yet in the old days women seemed to have babies out of wedlock without batting an eye. Look at Josephine and her lovers. And Napoleon's mistresses. Or maybe they did worry about getting pregnant. How could anyone know how they really felt? Unless they said so in their diaries.

"Who," asked Robert, "is the *Cosmopolitan* girl?" He had put his shorts back on.

"That female on the back page of the *Times*. You know, the one who runs barefoot through fields of men screaming about how sexy she is."

He looked dubious. "I don't think you're exactly the type. Of course," he added politely, "I've never seen her."

"Oh, Robert. I suppose you don't know the Peck and Peck woman, either."

He shook his head.

"She drives me up a wall. 'There is a certain kind of woman who would rather have her maid speak Sanskrit than cook.' I took a pledge. If I have to go naked, I won't get anything at Peck and Peck as long as *she* buys there."

"You're a nut, a lovely round nut."

"Just because the only paper you really read is *The Wall Street Journal*." She went to sit on the floor at his feet and leaned against his legs. She loved the way he felt. "I don't know how I ever got involved with a mixed-up, fair-weather liberal like you."

"Sex," he said smugly. "I'm very sexy."

She rubbed her cheek against his kneecap. "You're so bony, like a horse. If you broke your leg, you'd have to be shot. I don't think it's sex," she told him, "not only. I think I truly love you. I shouldn't say it, should I?" she said. "But it pleases me."

"You should say it. It pleases me, too." He never said he loved her. He could be tender, and he could leave her black and blue, but he never let the words slip out.

It was all right, though. She didn't mean it. She was just trying to pretty up her sudden lust, her blinding, dizzying, biting, scratching, unexpected lust. Was that what it was like for everyone else? Was it just that the blood-red curtain had lifted later than usual for her? Or was it something that happened to everyone at forty? "Do you think maybe I'm a nymphomaniac?" she asked Robert, mock-seriously, knowing it would divert him, and as she had expected, he grinned. "There are times," he said, groaning, and then he yanked away the towel and pulled her to him roughly.

She did love him. She had not expected to. Certainly she had not loved him when she decided to go to bed with him. She was still not quite sure how she had brought herself to do it, not loving him. He had just happened to be there at the right moment in time—her time. Another day, another moment, there might have been nothing at all.

In the beginning she used to caution herself against attaching any significance to the affair, either way. What difference did it make? Set against the real problems of Vietnam and the ghettos, with people struggling, starving, dying all over the world, what Molly Gilbert did or did not do was of profound unimportance. Even to her. But if anyone's personal life did mean anything, all that could be said was that she was an adult, it was her body, she could do as she pleased with it, provided she did not hurt anyone.

Besides it was ludicrous for her entire sexual experience to be limited to one man. Practically one man, anyhow. Even elementary curiosity called for more than that. There she sat, grandly dispensing advice, and in some ways she was more ignorant than the rawest teen-ager, than Barbara Jean probably. No, love had nothing at all to do with her sleeping with Robert.

But not for long. As soon as she went to bed with him, everything changed. Love had everything to do with it. What happened to her was what her secretary, Beth, had tried to explain that time.

Beth was twenty-six, a bright, gay, ambitious girl, with a personal life so varied that if she had been anyone else, Molly would have had to agree that she was promiscuous. With Beth, somehow, it was different. But when she got the agency to give Beth a stipend to go back for her degree in social work, Molly had felt an obligation to bring up the matter of Beth's young men with her, at least obliquely.

Beth gave her the opening when she announced that she had a new telephone number. Again. This time she was going to live in the East Village, with a songwriter.

"I'm puzzled," Molly had said frankly. "How can you be so sure this time when you were so positive each time before? And it turned into such a disaster?" How do you draw the line between love and promiscuity; how are you ever going to get anyone to marry you, my girl, if he can get you to bed without, and have you keep house besides, is what she wanted to ask, but she didn't want to hurt Beth, and anyhow, it was none of her business.

"I'm not sure," Beth said. "That's the point."

"That's why you're going to live with him? Because you're not sure how you feel about him?"

Beth nodded. "Of course. I have to know if it's just sex. I'm always meeting men I want to sleep with. Going to bed doesn't prove a thing. Not at first. You know how you always blow your mind in the beginning. It's when it goes on, and you find you like each other, too . . ."

"You mean you go to bed to find out if you're in love?"

"No. You go to bed to fall in love. If you're lucky, you do. Otherwise . . ."

"It sounds like *Through the Looking Glass*," commented Molly. Or, it struck her, like an old-fashioned arranged marriage. They got to know each other in bed. The only difference being that when it didn't work out, Beth picked herself up and went elsewhere. She didn't get stuck. Or was it her young man who didn't get stuck?

But she was no Beth, Molly realized. Here she was, lying beside a strange man on the ninth floor of the Toledo Hotel, and it made no difference whether she had convinced herself she was in love in order to justify going to bed, or whether going to bed begat loving, either way she was hooked. And she could not pick herself up and go elsewhere.

"Did you ever take a lie-detector test?" she asked Robert, idly.

He shook his head.

"I hate to lie," Molly said. "It makes me physically sick."

"You don't have to lie. You always think you have to explain everything. You don't. I never lie, and I don't give explanations. I just do what I have to do. What I want to do." He touched her face. "Don't be unhappy, Molly-o," he said. "You're a good woman."

"I'm a bad woman, but I don't care." She still could not understand it. Good little Molly, who always did what was expected of her. Molly, the constant wife. She and Mike had spent five weekends together, all told, the first three months they were married. Then he was sent to Karachi, and they did not see each other for over a year. In all that time, she had never so much as had lunch with another man. (Not that there were any young men left she would have liked to have lunch with that last year of the war, but even so . . .) It would have been inconceivable for her to go to bed with anyone else.

"Remember what I did with the diaphragm that time?" she started to ask Robert, and then, suddenly aware, stopped. How could he possibly remember? It had happened twenty-three years ago. The first weekend Mike had been scheduled to go overseas.

Mike had managed to get a pass. He was taking a midnight train back to camp. They had stopped at Jack Delaney's bar for a farewell drink—the man at the piano was playing "On the Sunny Side of the Street," she remembered—and then they went to Pennsylvania Station. She had watched him go down the big, double staircase to the Washington train and then, blank-eyed, like a Greek statue, she walked through the great vaulted waiting room to the subway and went home alone. In the morning, she removed her diaphragm (fitted some weeks before in the Planned Parenthood clinic by a square-shouldered, no-nonsense woman doctor in a heavy tweed suit), washed it carefully, wrapped it in a paper napkin and deposited it in the garbage pail. ("Golden Gate in Forty-eight" was what the soldiers were saying, as they left San Francisco. What was the point of saving it for so long?) Then she cried.

The next week, Mike was back, his shipping orders delayed. She smiled, recalling how disconcerted he had been when she told him what she had done with the diaphragm, and started to tell Robert about it, and then realized she couldn't tell him that either. Or explain to him how, for a moment back there in 1944, he and Mike had been one and the same person.

It was then that Robert reached over her to the night table and picked up his watch. "Time," he said. "You have to make dinner tonight, don't you?"

She was overwhelmed that he remembered. Arletta never came in on Wednesday. It was her day to sleep late. She cleaned the church in the afternoon.

"I've got to get going, too," he added. "We're having a party. Black tie. Jane thinks people are less boring when they dress."

Molly got up quickly. They never discussed Jane or Mike, but they never pretended they did not exist, either. Robert occasionally inquired about Mike's project, and he mentioned Jane casually and amiably, and every time he did so, Molly felt a wave of nausea. When she thought of them together, it was like wrenching open a wound.

Back in the bathroom, she leaned over the basin and observed herself in the mirror with scorn. She was crazy. All he wanted of her was servicing. Ego-building. He was insatiable. A stud.

She pulled the towel off her head and tried to get her hair back into shape. What could she make for dinner, at this hour? There was probably enough meat left over from yesterday. Arletta still cooked as if David was home, but she would have to stop for milk.

"Robert," she called out, "do you suppose Héloise went marketing in the afternoon after she went to bed with Abelard?"

"They were married. Don't you remember?" He came into the bathroom, zipped up the back of her dress and fastened the top hook expertly. "The only trouble was he was a priest."

For the moment her longing was so great she had to close her eyes and bite her lips to keep from saying anything. He could see her face in the mirror, but she couldn't help it. Every day found her closer to the edge of the pit.

The night before she had awakened in a cold sweat from a dream in which she was driving along a beach road and came upon a corpse lying on a dune with a full moon above it. All it needs to be a Rousseau is a lion, she thought, in the dream, and then a voice had said coldly, "There is a lion. You."

The daydreams were worse. Usually Jane vanished somehow—entered a nunnery, maybe, or died quickly and easily of something dreadful she never knew she had, so that her death came as a blessing, and Robert, accompanied by the children, would come and plead with her to marry him. (Mike had vanished, too, equally painlessly.) The trouble was she didn't want to live with Robert's children. It would be easy enough for him. All she had was David, and he was not home any more. But Robert had the three, they were still young, he doted on them, and they sounded impossible. Demanding and spoiled, except for Mary. She could probably take Mary. Or was it only that Mary was so difficult that she presented no threat? Was that why Molly wasn't jealous of her?

Enough.

Robert was ready to leave. "Tuesday? I'm clear in the afternoon."

"I don't know." Never, if she had anything to say about it, never again. "There may be a staff meeting." She hated herself in the evening, and in the morning, and every minute in between.

"I'll call you."

She nodded, and he left.

A LOVING WIFE

"Whore," she said into the mirror.

"But I love him," the drawn face replied. "Doesn't that make a difference?"

"No," Molly told herself, "it does not."

CHAPTER 5

         It was always like that. Each time she went to bed with Robert, she vowed it would be the last. It was not as though she were deprived sexually, or mistreated. She did not have to live with impotence, sadism, masturbation, homosexuality, or demands so bizarre that when distraught clients described them, she was more astonished than horrified (as well as aware, of course, that very often it was fantasy, not reality, that was the perversion). Mike was not unfaithful, or if he was, she didn't know it, which amounted to the same thing, and over the years they had worked out a predictably satisfactory physical relationship. Judging from her still-limited experience, all men were certainly not alike, but they were alike enough. The difference lay in the reaction they evoked.

It was nothing intrinsic. It was like looking at an Abstract Expressionist painting. It wasn't what was there so much as what you brought to it. The rest was periphery. Was the world well lost for periphery? Of course not.

Then she would hear Robert's voice on the telephone, and she was eighteen again, walking on new grass, wracked with bittersweet longing.

"Lunch tomorrow?"

"Yes." She breathed through slivers of glass.

"Fine. See you then."

The dam broke. She wanted to whirl around the room, press herself against the wall, embrace the chair. Instead she walked quietly out to the files and found a report Robert had signed and ran her fingers over the signature. Next thing I know, she thought, I'll be writing our names down, one over the other—what a lovely Freudian idea, crossing out the O's and B's to see if it comes out that he loves me.

When she left the office, she hurried down the street, singing softly, but unaware, so that people turned around and smiled. Away from Robert, she lived a half-life, but on the surface, her days seemed more whole than ever; her happiness overflowed, filling every visible crack. For once, time was like an accordion, stretching to suit her needs. Nothing was too much for her. Hours darted by on wings, her heart raced in double-time. She should have been tired, she slept so fitfully, but she was not, she was exhilarated. She was not even angry any more when Mike woke her with his insomnia. He had been doing it now for years. She could not remember when it began. One year he had been sleeping until noon, the next he was up before dawn. He awoke like a child, confident the world came alive with him. He tripped over chairs, creaked closet doors, flushed toilets, rustled scientific journals, while she pretended sleep, throat rigid with resentment, remembering how quietly she remained in bed, her thoughts scurrying about restlessly, on the rare occasions when she woke up first. But now she welcomed the secret wakeful hours. She lay on her stomach, thinking of Robert, burning and rejoicing, and no one could see her face.

Actually she and Mike never got along better than they did then. She was so conscious of the wrong she was doing him, she went out of her way to please him. She remembered to have his shoes repaired, canceled engagements at the last minute if he felt like staying home (or going to the movies), planned dinner for eight o'clock and served it cheerfully at ten when he forgot to look at the lab clock. She listened when he wanted to talk and was still when he brooded. He could go his own way all day and reach for her without a word as soon as he turned out his light, and still she did not resent it. How could she? She was in love with the whole world, her husband included. She ought to write a letter to the *Ladies Home Journal*—"How My Marriage Was Saved." "It was easy, doctor, I took a lover."

But if Robert did not call when she expected him to,

she turned to lead. She became a prisoner at her desk, reluctant to leave even for a moment for fear she would miss him if he did telephone. Food stuck in her throat. She grew numb with dread that at last she was getting what she deserved. He was tired of her. He had suddenly seen her for what she was—a faintly ridiculous, mildly overweight, middle-aged romantic with delusions of adolescence. He had another woman.

She told him about her panics finally.

"I even called you on Thursday," she confessed. "I thought I'd hear you say hello and then hang up. But a maid answered." It wasn't a maid, it was Jane, she was sure of it, but she could not bring herself to tell him so. "I gave a wrong number."

Next day when she got to her office, there was a small package on her desk. It contained a blue-glazed, mummy-shaped clay figure with a smudged Egyptian face and a card written in a firm, black hand: "This is a *shawabty*, from a very minor tomb. The inscription says: 'If you call, I will answer.' And so I will—through eternity."

"It isn't worth much," Robert assured her later. He kept wanting to buy her presents, but Molly wouldn't let him. "They're all over Cairo. There must be millions of them around. Any Egyptian above the rank of servant had to be buried with enough of these to take care of any menial job he might have to do in his afterlife."

The week after he gave her the *shawabty*, he stopped calling again, but this time she needed no talisman to reassure her. She knew where he was—in Canada, with

Jane and the children, skiing from Christmas to after New Year's. They always went away for the holidays; the parties they would have to give or go to otherwise made Robert frantic. It was unsettling to think about, but it was just as well he was away. She couldn't have seen him anyhow, she was swamped.

As always, she had taken some time off during David's Christmas vacation, but she still found it hard to keep up with all she had to do at home. It was true David's girl was there, too, but Susan didn't make that much difference. Molly had simply forgotten how demanding it was to work and take care of a family. Looking back she found it hard to imagine how she had managed it.

Perhaps it was because she had never known anything else. She had finished getting her degree while Mike was in the army, and then went right to work. Even when David was born, she stayed away only long enough to make sure that Evelyn, who was going to take care of him, understood some of the ramifications of Spock, Gesell, and Ilg. It was her own choice, she reminded herself, thinking back. Mike had nothing to do with it. It was not a matter of money either, and then, as usual, she asked herself whom she was kidding. They couldn't possibly have lived the way they did without her salary. Mike raced through his doctorate, but it took him two more years after he got back, all the same. By the time he was set at the Institute, they had become accustomed to private schools and country weekends. Research alone would have paid for a nice little house in Hartsdale.

Maybe it would have been different if she had had more children, but she hadn't. The baby would have been—"was," she corrected herself—a girl. The obstetrician told her it was dead when she went for her six-month's checkup. One of those things, a fluke. "We can do a Caesarian," he had said, "but if you can stand it, I'd like to let nature take its course. Then you only have to give yourself a month or two before you start another one." She walked around for five more weeks with a dead infant under her heart. She went to work every day and came home at night and played with David and put him to bed. Then, just as the doctor had promised, she went into labor and easily, naturally, was delivered. It was all very beautiful and right, she agreed serenely afterward, and she took care never to let herself become pregnant again.

Did Mike mind her working? Not at all. He would have been disappointed in her if she had stopped. He had barely concealed contempt for what he called "women who stayed home and eat bonbons." He was a Lucy Stoner at heart. He wanted Molly to be fulfilled, he used to say when they were younger. She had had the best of two worlds, a family and a career.

It meant, of course, that she had never had a moment when she could relax. She lived according to a timetable, but an uncertain one, in a perpetual state of revision. Measles, meetings, maids quitting—all bore the threat of collision and derailment. She played with schedules like a juggler. If there was an open house for her to go to at David's school, she skipped lunch twice. If she had to hear Anna Freud speak on a Saturday, she got tickets for a game at Yankee Stadium and dropped David and a friend off first. She never asked Mike to take over for her, nor did she want him to. It was not enough for her to be a good mother; she had to be a little more devoted than anyone else, simply to prove that she worked for positive reasons, not because she could not make a go of it at home.

(She had never quite convinced herself. Alice Barnes, mother of David's best friend in the lower school, who had been given to thanking her "lucky stars" that she didn't "have" to work, used to say that "working outside is for cowards, it gives you an excuse to avoid anything you don't want to do." Deep down, Molly was always afraid that Alice might be right. On the other hand, Alice had blandly refused to learn to drive, even though the Barneses lived in Riverdale then. "Why should I?" she had said. "I'd be nothing but a chauffeur." Oh, well. Let he who is without sin . . .)

Then there was the matter of roles. Molly was very careful to see that David was not confused about who was who in his family. Whether she worked or not, she wanted David to think of her domestically, not as a peer of his father's. So far as she could tell, he did, too. (For years she had had scotch-taped on her office wall a drawing of David's entitled "My Mother and My Father." It showed a large, amorphous figure peering into what might have been a microscope and a small, equally amorphous figure holding an obvious broom. Molly always felt reassured at the sight of it.) It helped, of course, that Mike had no conflict about his masculinity. As a matter of fact, when Angela first said she wanted her to be assistant director, Molly told her she would love the job, but she would have to think about it. "I don't want to drown Mike," she had explained. "Drown him?" said Angela. "You can't even swim!" There were times when Molly wished Mike did feel threatened. Like Bernie Silver who never used to let Debbie go anywhere alone at night, not even to a PTA meeting. "It's all right if I call for her," Molly once complained to Mike. "It doesn't seem to matter if I'm in a taxi alone. Do you ever worry about me?" "Of course not," he assured her. "I know you can take care of yourself." Debbie never appeared at breakfast, practiced yoga religiously, and had her hair done twice a week, and Molly had been fiercely envious of her, as she was of all women who seemed to feel no need to earn their keep, who thought it was enough for them to be what they were. Female. Period. If only once Mike had demanded that she stay home . . . Enough, she told herself sternly. Let's not go overboard. If he ever had asked you to quit, you would have been devastated. You love what you do.

It was true. Each day, when she walked into the office, she hung up her conflict like a coat. She was her own woman, well at ease. Elevator men smiled at her, Beth adored her, the caseworkers she supervised re-

spected her, she got along well with Angela. At the
Center, she knew who she was—a successful human being, working within a framework of hours and days,
subject to a discipline that was outer as well as inner.
She had tangible proof of her worth—evaluations, pro-
motions, consultations, gratitude, tenure, and a pay-
check. Whereas at home, life was a maze of questions.
Was she really a good mother? Would the Bartons and
Friedmans be good together, or should she make it
cocktails and supper and invite three or four other
couples as buffer? Was Mike giving her freedom or
simply dumping responsibility on her?

Most of the questions had ended, of course, when
David went off to college. There were fewer responsi-
bilities, less to be guilty about. Besides, everyone she
knew seemed to be working, or desperate to work,
even Alice Barnes and Debbie Silver. Women weren't
guilty about working any more anyhow; they were
more likely to be guilty if they didn't work. And truthfully, she managed better than most. She had had more
practice, and a better job.

But whenever David turned up, it was like the old
days again. The apartment came alive, record player
booming, refrigerator door slamming, papers and books
scattered everywhere, the hall bathroom turned into
a sauna with the steam from David's half-hour showers.
Her life fell apart. She never made any plans during
his vacations, because while it was impossible to tell
when David would be staying home, she was eager to
be there when he did. She never knew how many

would be sitting down to meals. The apartment was like a magnet for David's suburban friends—it was the reward, Molly supposed, for the deprivations of a city childhood—and they arrived at all hours, being nocturnal as well as ravenous. When Arletta grumbled, Molly tried to point out how hard they had it at school. She made Portland sound rather like a prison camp, but Arletta was never convinced. Fortunately, vacation always seemed to end at the exact moment Arletta seemed to have made up her mind once and for all to take her old shoes with her and depart for good.

CHAPTER 6

David and Susan turned up the Wednesday before Christmas, a day earlier than they had said they would.

Mike had gone back to check on some tests they were running at the lab, and Molly was making out menus for the coming week when the doorbell rang. She was delighted to see them, and slightly taken aback, too, since the refrigerator was still unstocked. She was going to call in her order the next day. To tell the truth, she hadn't given David's coming much thought this time. She was too involved with herself.

"We're starved," David said.

"They served dinner on the plane, but it was horrible," Susan amplified. "Even I cook better than that." She looked like a pretty, medieval page with her straight, short-cropped yellow hair. Or a downy little chicken.

Molly led the way to the kitchen. "I'll see what there is," she said apologetically. "Did school close earlier than you expected?"

"No," said David, "we cut today's classes. We had it."

"*You* had it," Susan corrected him. "I was supposed to get my philosophy paper back today," she told Molly. "I was really dying to see what I got. But His Highness said no, so here we are." She sounded like an aggrieved wife.

"You can't win, Susan," said Molly, enjoying it. It was going to be nice to have a daughter-in-law some-day. "You might as well get used to it. How about a cheese omelette?" As usual, she had already broken the eggs before she asked the question. It was a bad habit of hers, she knew, offering choices when she had already made irrevocable decisions. Unfortunately, she usually realized it after it was too late to do anything about it. It was an outgrowth of her need to please, she supposed, but inexcusable all the same. Fortu-nately, she was not often caught. "He's just like his fa-ther," she said now quickly, covering up, "stubborn. If you were the one who had wanted to cut classes . . ."

"Oh, he would have cut them," Susan interrupted. "Of course he would have." She sounded surprised that Molly should assume otherwise. They chatted amiably until after eleven. When it became apparent that this was going to be another one of Mike's nights, Molly said they had better not wait up for him. "I guess you're not tired, though," she said. "It's earlier in Portland, isn't it?"

"Oh, no, I'm beat," Susan said. "When was it we started packing, David?"

"Four o'clock this morning. That's when you finished typing, wasn't it?" He turned to Molly. "I finally got my report on Beckett done. Last night. Toward the end, Susan was typing as I wrote."

"Good," said Molly. He had been struggling with it since last semester, she knew. She went to the linen closet and got sheets for the couch in the old dining area which Mike now used as a study. "I'll leave a note for Arletta, David," she said idly, as she passed through the living room, "so she doesn't burst in on you and wake you up."

David got up from the floor where he had been sorting records, re-establishing old friendships, and followed her. "What are you doing?" He acted bewildered.

"Making up your bed." He was really unbelievably selfish, Molly decided, deeply disappointed in him. "I know you'd like to have your own room," she added coldly, "but you can't expect Susan to sleep out in the open like this. After all, it isn't her house."

He shook his head in amazement. "I just don't understand you."

Now Molly was bewildered. "What do you mean?"

"Why does anyone have to sleep here? There are two beds in my room, aren't there?" He had started

71

out shouting, but at the expression on her face, he lowered his voice. "Mom," he said, almost gently, "you
know we have an apartment together in Portland."

Molly knew Susan answered the telephone most of
the time when she called David. She had sent them a
tin box of Arletta's brownies and a joint subscription
to *The New York Review of Books.* "Well," she began,
and then she stopped. There was really nothing she
could say.

Susan strolled over and David put an arm around
her shoulder. Obviously she had overheard. "Maybe
your mother would feel more comfortable if I slept in
here," she told David reasonably. "I don't mind." She
seemed totally unperturbed.

"It's not that," said Molly. "It's just . . ."

"Just what?" David looked like a small boy whose
mother had just embarrassed him by stopping a base-
ball game to make him put on a sweater.

"What will Arletta think?" At last Molly knew what
had been troubling her.

"Arletta!" He hooted.

"She's hardly the one, is she?" commented Molly,
and after a moment, she and David began to laugh. She
pulled the sheet off the couch and folded it slowly
while Susan picked up the top sheet, the blanket, and
the pillow. "Where shall I put these, Mrs. Gilbert?"

"Back in the linen closet. In the hall." Molly was
both upset and regretful. She had made a fool of herself, and she had embarrassed them. Then, comforting herself, she tried to imagine what her mother

would have done in a similar situation. But it could never have happened with her mother. She had never even felt free enough to so much as hold hands with a boy in front of her.

The sheets disposed of, Susan returned and touched her tentatively, as if she wanted to say something, but then she settled for a murmured good night, went into David's room and closed the door firmly behind her. David lingered. He, too, seemed to want to say something but was apparently unable to make a start.

"I know I'm inconsistent," Molly said, after a while, helping him. "The funny thing is, I really approve. It's much more honest." It was, too, she thought. There was an openness about David and Susan and their relationship together that she and Mike still had not achieved, after all these years. Even the way they dressed—or didn't dress—showed it. Susan was not poor (her father was an executive in some oil company, Molly surmised, from the way she described him), but as far as Molly could tell, her worldly possessions could be fitted into a knapsack. At least, that was all she ever carried with her. She did not need clothes to woo David. There was no coquetry in her. She rarely even put on eye makeup. She was sure to turn up for breakfast wearing an old flannel nightgown—or one of David's old shirts. It was as though, having committed herself wholly, she no longer felt the need to be anything but herself, Susan, bare.

"I guess so," said David.

"Healthier, too," Molly said. "Psychologically, I

mean," she added quickly. Good Lord, she thought, that was a narrow escape. Although the other was true, too, don't think it wasn't.

What was it they used to do when she was young? Sit on camp cots and discuss whether it was all right to kiss on the second date? (It was unthinkable on the first, of course.) It was more a matter of ethics than of sexual urgency. Boys didn't take girls anywhere any more, a big evening seemed to consist of a six-pack of beer and a stack of records (or a few joints, Molly noted, adjuring herself not to be naïve). But when someone strapped himself for a night at Nick's or a fraternity house "formal," gardenia, souvenir compact, and all, wasn't he entitled to more than a handshake at the end? Even if he turned out to be a creep?

That stage past, they used to neck tirelessly in the backs of cars until three or four o'clock in the morning. Or pet. The difference was not semantic. There was probably more platonic dialogue about going "below the shoulders" or remaining above them than was dreamed of in the "Phaedo." ("We must have been frigid," Molly marveled, recalling those nights, "or else boys used to be impotent.")

Finally, emancipated, they reached a peak of "going steady," and anything went, so long as virginity survived technically intact. They became experts at making short stops, a skill that sometimes had interesting ramifications later when they married and the flashing red lights were supposed to go off. (Didn't Flossie, her college roommate, once actually go away with a man for a weekend and return chaste? "Wasn't it kind of teasing?" Molly remembered asking tentatively, and Flossie had retorted: "Well, he couldn't expect me to go all the way, could he?")

"You don't use each other," Molly told her son now. "You really care about each other."

"Sure, Mom."

"It's not your living together that counts," she went on. "It's the quality of your relationship. It's more open, meaningful . . ." What crap, she thought, what unadulterated crap. I sound more and more like Angela every minute. Why am I so nervous?

But David seemed pleased. They were on familiar ground. His mother was making hot chocolate with marshmallows for everyone now that the ball game was over. "That's exactly the point," he said.

"It's as though you were married really."

"Well," he said dubiously. He hesitated for a moment and then apparently decided it was too much after all. Those marshmallows—everyone really hated them. "Marriage has nothing to do with it, you know, Mom. I don't even know if we'll ever be married. Right now, it's what it is. Us together, here, now, because we want to be. That's all."

"I don't understand." She really didn't.

David frowned. "Well, you seem to see everything in a straight line. People going out with each other, shopping around, everything on a trial basis, even sleeping together. You accept that all right, but only because you think of it as testing for the right combination. When you find it, you're supposed to stop right where you are and pair up for good. Everything has to get somewhere."

"Doesn't it?" Then what was she doing clearly rushing toward nowhere?

"Why? Why can't it just be?" He was obviously just groping. "I can't put my finger on it," he said, "but it's like 'The Farmer in the Dell' with you. You know, everything all set—'the farmer takes the wife, the wife takes the child . . .'" He smiled at her. "Kind of naïve, Mom."

Naïve is as naïve does, she thought, wryly. Nothing is as complicated as "The Farmer in the Dell," my boy. It can even turn out to be *Oedipus*. Isn't that what *Oedipus* comes down to in the end? The wife takes the child? Or should it be "the wife takes a lover"?

She frowned then, and David, misunderstanding the look on her face, said hurriedly: "I didn't mean to be insulting, Mom. I don't mean you're all wrong. It's just that you act as if marriage is the only happy ending."

"Isn't it?" For Susan, if not for him, she wanted to add, but she suddenly felt too protective of Susan to say it.

"I don't think so. Not right now, anyhow. The way I see it, there are lots of possibilities. There are all kinds of choices. Whether a given choice is good or bad depends entirely on the people involved, or on their own particular situation. Their time of life."

He had a point but she wasn't sure he knew it. "How does marriage fit in?"

"If you want to have children, you get married. That goes without saying. At least, in our society."

"And how about—what you call choices—after you're married? When you're older," she added mischievously.

"Oh," he said airily, "by that time . . ."

We're too decrepit to care, thought Molly. She was both amused and deflated. "You didn't really think he had all the answers, did you?" she asked herself. She started to say something, but at that point David gave a loud yawn. He kissed her cheek lightly and patted her shoulder. "Good night, Mom." He bolted down the hall and then he, too, closed the door behind him.

Molly was still awake when Mike came in. It was half past twelve, and he was clearly exhausted. "David's here," she said. "They're sleeping in his room."

"Oh," he said, "I thought they were coming tomorrow."

"They came early."

He went into the bathroom and when he came out again, she still had her light on. He looked at her for a moment, puzzled. "Anything the matter?"

"I said they're sleeping in David's room."

"Where else could you put them?"

"You think it's all right?" He always surprised her.

"Well," he said offhandedly, "why not? Why is it different here than in Portland?" He gave a little laugh. "Let her family worry."

Exactly. "That's not the point," she said angrily. She took a deep breath and made the attempt. Maybe,

maybe just this once, she could get him to pay attention. To discuss. To care. "Intellectually, I'm all for it,
but emotionally, here, in my own house . . ."

"You're a square," Mike said kindly. "They're young,
Molly. They have hot pants. You've got to be a little
more understanding. Sex doesn't have any rules."

"You don't think so?"

"No." He flipped off his light. "If you don't mind," he
said, yawning, "I'm beat."

It was a difficult week. She found their presence
literally unbearable. Walking past their closed door in
the morning she shook with longing for Robert. Once,
David, struck by the sheer joy of being alive, seized her
unexpectedly, and to her discomfiture and amusement,
she felt a quick, classic flick of desire. He was all sperm
and sweat, her young man, she noted. How is it she
had never been aware of it before? They left at last on
New Year's Day, and the next day, gratefully, she went
back to work. She was barely in her office when the
telephone rang.

It was Robert.

"I thought you weren't coming home until tomorrow night," she said.

"I made up a telephone call. I said I had to get back.
Jane and the kids are coming home tomorrow."

She tried to keep the rapture out of her voice. "You
shouldn't have done it."

"I had to," he said. "I was going nuts not seeing
you."

CHAPTER 7

She never told her love, but it was certainly there for all to see, thought Molly. It was either a miracle or an example of how little attention people really paid to each other that no one apparently noticed. It was written all over her, she knew, just as she was sure it had been long ago, after that first time, when she was a girl and terrified of coming in to breakfast the next morning and facing her parents.

If nothing else, she wondered now, stuffing two folders into a manila envelope (hopefully, she would be able to go over them tonight), how was it possible for her to leave afternoons like this without once someone making a comment?

She walked past Angela's office and waved at her, daring fate. Angela waved back. "Work well, my dear," she said mysteriously.

Molly had tried to figure out what Angela meant all the way to the Toledo. Just as she got there, it hit her. Angela thought she was seeing a psychiatrist. The idea would please her. "You see," Angela would tell herself, "marriage doesn't solve everything." That would be her explanation for Molly's recent moods—Angela was too sensitive not to have been aware of them. Tension and release. Angela understood, Angela was accepting. Well? That's what it amounted to, didn't it? Tension and release.

She went up to their room and waited. Tense. But when Robert arrived, she took one look at him and burst out laughing. "How could we?" she gasped, wiping away tears.

"I don't know," he said, and broke up too.

The last time they had been together was on the floor of his office, in the dark, behind his desk. Afterwards—at least it was afterwards—his foot had knocked the metal wastebasket against the chrome legs of the leather swivel chair which had been pushed away to make room. It made a clanging sound, and with one accord, they had crawled into the alcove of the desk, hands against each other's mouths to keep from laughing aloud, hiding in case the night watchman should come to investigate. He would have found them anyhow, of course. Their coats and shoes were on the Bokhara rug in front of the desk. But they were too joyously besotted to remember.

By happy coincidence, Mike and Jane, both, were out that night, so they had been able to have dinner together for the first time, at an obscure Scandinavian restaurant downtown. The waiter's suggested apéritif, aquavit with a beer chaser, proved so pleasing they had several more, with the result that they had reeled out of the restaurant with but one thought in mind.

"Did I ever tell you," Molly had said, "about the couple we met in Paris once? They came from Milwaukee. They had six children. I guess they must have been in their late forties. Do you know how they were spending their week in Paris? Going to all the striptease places. As soon as they felt high enough, they'd hop a cab and rush back to their hotel. We sat next to them at some café, and they told us about it. I thought they were mad."

"Sounds great to me."

"Doesn't it?"

He had hailed a cab.

"Where are we going?" asked Molly.

"The Ritz. Or do you prefer the Crillon?" He leaned forward and gave the driver his office address. When they got there, the night elevator man took them to the fortieth floor without batting an eye.

Wasn't it strange, Molly thought now, how acceptable everything seemed when you yourself did it? If she had found two people coupling behind her desk—or God forbid, if Robert had found a clerk and a secretary behind *his*—it was like the time she and Adam were upstairs in the dark at a fraternity house party, without realizing, until they heard some sounds, after a while, that there was another couple on the other side of the room. Disgusting, had been her first reaction. It's different with us, was her second. What we do is beautiful.

What she and Robert did was beautiful, too, always, anywhere, even in hotel rooms.

"Was everything all right when you got in Wednesday morning?" she asked Robert now.

"Same as always, except these were on my desk." He held up her beige leather gloves. She had missed them when they were going uptown again and he had given her his gloves to wear. She had them in her purse now, and she had no intention of giving them back. She slipped them on at odd times of the day when she was sure no one was looking. They felt like a caress.

"Oh, my," said Molly. "Who do you suppose found them?"

"What difference does it make?"

If it didn't matter to him, it certainly didn't matter to her, but she felt vaguely annoyed.

He took off his tie and she hung up her dress.

"Do they still put out those books with the best plays of the year, do you know?" she asked.

"I don't know. I never heard of them."

"Oh, Robert, you must have seen them. I used to get them out of the library all the time when I was a kid. They were marvelous. Chunky little black-bound books with all the best scenes of each year's plays in them. They had bits of dialogue and little summaries of the action in each one. I used to read the dialogue aloud to myself."

"Uh-uh. Don't know them."

"The editor was a little old man in a wing collar. At least, that's how I always pictured him. A kind of benign Henry James. Burns Mantle it was. You won't believe it, but he worked for the *Daily News*."

"So that's what you did when you were a kid." He smiled at her, and she thought no one had ever looked at her so lovingly before.

"Oh, I jumped horses and played squash and tried out for the singles at Wimbledon, too," she assured him.

"Don't be fresh," he said. "What made you think of the Best Plays just now?"

"We saw *America Hurrah!* last night. Have you seen it yet?"

He shook his head.

"I was just wondering what my little old man would have made of it."

"We haven't seen much off-Broadway. I think the last one was *The Balcony*. Jane wouldn't come back after the intermission."

"I don't blame her," said Molly. "It made me feel dirty. Not sex-dirty. Just plain dirty. It was a dirty play, like *Marat-Sade*. We sat so close the actors were spitting at us, and their costumes were so filthy I was afraid things were going to start crawling on me."

It was how she felt now, queasy, just as she had the night before when those two balloon-shaped dolls undressed in the glare of lights in the motel-room sequence of *America Hurrah!* It's different with us, she had thought then, flushing. We're not like that at all. But she was glad for the darkness that hid her face. That was what she was really thinking of, those monstrous dolls, not the Best American Plays. Her guilt had broken out of its cage again.

"What's the matter, Molly-o?" Robert asked, seeing her expression.

"Nothing."

"Something," he insisted. "What is it?"

"What else?"

He sat down and removed his shoes. "Don't be a barefoot girl, Molly," he said. "We have the best of each other. You know it; I know it. No new cars that break down, no relatives to placate, you're not putting rollers in your hair when I want you to come to bed, the children aren't prowling in the hall . . ."

"Or not calling when they said they would. It never ends." She smiled bleakly. "I can't even fall asleep Sunday nights because I'm afraid—hoping, that is—David will call. If he calls at all, it's on Sunday. He tends to call on the spur of the moment, and he forgets about the time, so if he feels like talking around midnight, it'll be three o'clock in the morning here, and I'm so afraid I'll sound groggy . . ."

Robert was incredulous. "You're afraid you'll sound groggy? I wouldn't even answer the telephone at that hour. Not for the Pope himself."

"But I want to talk to him," she said, and he said: "I know you do," and took her in his arms.

"We could talk all day, couldn't we," she said gladly, and he said: "No, no, no, we couldn't."

Her guilt really did not escape against her will, she thought later, released. It was more like a pet that she took out and exercised, out of duty. Otherwise, she ignored it. The scratches it inflicted barely broke the skin. They were purely for show. "See," she could say, "see how bruised I am. You don't have to punish me. I'm punished already."

Who would punish her? Jane. She had become obsessed with Jane. They had all bumped into each other unexpectedly two weeks before at *Man of La Mancha.* She and Robert had greeted each other pleasantly and made the appropriate introductions. Then they had parted. (They had seen each other three times since then but, curiously, neither had mentioned the meeting.) It was the first time Molly had seen Jane. She was not at all what she had pictured. Molly had thought of her as looking like Robert, as tall, as dark, and as imperious. Like an arrogant hawk. But she was actually only moderately tall, sandy blond and rather pretty. Wiry, too, like a woman dedicated to tennis.

With features now attached to the previously faceless dark Fury of her imagination, Molly thenceforth saw Jane everywhere she turned. She saw her coming down the street, in the next dressing room at

85

Bloomingdale's, in a passing car, under the dryer at the hairdresser's.

Every time she and Mike went out, she was in terror of walking into a room and seeing Robert there with Jane. It could have happened. It turned out that they did have mutual friends. But it was not likely. Still, Molly took to asking, "Who else are you having?" whenever they were asked to dinner, a question she always resented somehow when it was asked of her. What she would have done if her hostess had answered, "The Singers. Do you know them?", she had no idea. Anyhow, she suspected she yearned to be in the same room with them as much as she feared it. Besides, even if Jane did find out, it was not likely she would confront her publicly. But then, who could tell? Wasn't it Bea Rogers, prim, shy almost to the point of rudeness, who took to appearing at the advertising agency where her husband worked and upbraiding his secretary? As Molly had heard it, she came in shouting "Whore" one day and "Homewrecker" the next, and never once got mixed up and uttered the same epithet twice in a row.

Enough, Molly ordered herself, change the subject. Stop wallowing.

She thought of the Best Plays again. They had reposed in a row on the second shelf from the bottom in the dimly lit back room of the public library, she recalled. The library had a special smell, a mixture of shellacked wood and antiseptic dust. A good smell. There was always a stool in the essay/play section, and she usually sat and read a little of a book before

she took it out. What was the name of the play she
had loved so much? *Reunion in Vienna,* that was it.
For years she had been under the impression that she
had seen it, but she never had. She had simply read
it over and over again in the Best Plays. Lynn Fontanne was in it, and who else? Alfred Lunt—it had to
be Alfred Lunt. She could see the faded, grayish,
rotogravure photograph in the book right now. Husband in one corner, lover in the other, Fontanne, head
thrown back and long graceful arm outstretched,
pointing to an empty space between them, where her
ideal man would be. Was there really such a picture,
or did Molly imagine it?

At any rate, that's how she felt now. Somewhere in
the middle, between Robert and Mike, was the man
for her. Mike was so involved in what he did that he
made her feel like a satellite, a sort of Saturn's ring,
held in place only by the gravity of marriage. But
Robert's lack of commitment made him somehow
lightweight, so that, in the end, it was inconceivable
to think of revolving about him at all.

Feeling as if she had just betrayed him in her
thoughts, Molly now felt guilty toward Robert. She
reached out a protective hand and, as she touched
him, suddenly was open-mouthed with longing again.

❀

In February, Jane went to Palm Springs for her an-
nual visit with her parents. The two weeks she was
gone were the happiest days of Molly's life.

CHAPTER 8

She and Mike began quarreling—really quarreling, that is—sometime in March.

The first big flare-up was probably the one on the Triborough Bridge. The incident that sparked it was as trifling as the ones that were to follow. She said he was tailgating, he said he wasn't, she said she would get out of the car if he didn't stop it. They had argued all the way to Quogue, and then barely spoke all weekend. Her charge that he was constitutionally hostile—and a terrible driver besides—bewildered him. After all, he had been dogging the car in front of him for the last twenty years, and she had never even mentioned it before. Molly knew she was being unreasonable, but she couldn't stop herself. Anyway, it was true. He was a hostile driver.

The honeymoon is over, she had thought wryly,
making the first move toward civility Sunday night.
She still felt guilty about her affair, but not so guilty
that she was impelled to cook mussels for Mike or
admire his photographs effusively. A hair shirt, it appeared, was like a cast on a broken leg. Eventually,
you got so used to it the only time you were aware of
it was when it was removed.

Barriers down, they now seemed to bicker inces-
santly. They argued about the laundry putting starch
in collars, about food, a lost magazine, Dean Rusk,
and how much (if at all) the radiators should be
turned on. He called her interpretation of civil rights
juvenile; she informed him he lacked imagination. He
said it was disgraceful that David had no idea of what
he wanted to do when he got out of school and she
accused him of trying to run David's life for him.

In a way, it was almost better when they quarreled
because otherwise they seemed to have nothing to say
to each other. Mike was not given to small talk. He
made wisecracks, or discoursed on politics. Occasionally he asked Molly's opinion about a staff matter, and
every once in a while he gave vent to his disgust at
having to water down a federally supported project
so that it would be directed toward immediate ap-
plication instead of pure research.

But he never talked about his own work any more,
and Molly no longer asked him about it. He always
cut her off, as if the terms in which it might be discussed were beyond her comprehension. And yet in

the early days, when he first got started with steroids, he had been so excited, so overjoyed, at the possibilities he saw that he used to lecture her far into the night, drawing diagrams, sketching ramifications, leaving her dizzy with awe. (It was true that when she woke up the next morning she had no idea of what he had been talking about, but at least she had had the sense of sharing in what he was thinking—of looking through a very small telescope at a universe starry with promise.)

He was no longer interested in what she did, either. He used to be fascinated by the stories she brought home, unerring in his ability to put his finger at the dead center of a problem. They made a good pair, a useful, contributing pair, she used to think, holding the knowledge over everyone else's head like a secret weapon. Their minds were different, but in balance, and in everything that was basic, they were in solid agreement.

Where had it all gone?

If she started to tell him an anecdote now, he listened for a moment and then his attention strayed so obviously her voice would falter and what she had to say would trail off into gibberish.

Or he would listen, and his response would be so impatient she felt like a fool. That was what had triggered their fight about civil rights. It had actually begun when she told him how furious she was with Barbara Jean's high school. (Sandy had persuaded the village school board to accept her as a special student in light of her high I.Q.)

"They put her on probation just because she didn't get a couple of term papers in on time," Molly had told Mike.

"What's wrong with that?"

She had stared at him. "Well, in the first place, she's had no experience doing anything on time. Then, she's had to adjust to Oak Hollow, and a suburban school, and being the only Negro in her class. She may be the only one in the whole school, for all I know. Besides, it will make it harder for her to get into college."

"It'll be harder for her to get into college if they don't put her on probation," Mike said. "That's the trouble with you bleeding hearts. You're really racists at heart. You believe in two classes of citizenship. You have two standards, one for whites, and one for Negroes."

It was not so much what he said as the antagonistic tone in which he said it. "That's not the point," she said angrily. "All that I'm saying is that if the school takes her, it should at least give her a chance, work with her caseworker, give her time to get used to a whole new way of life. It's like taking someone from the jungle and expecting him to run a computer right away. It's not fair."

"It's not fair to expect him to run a computer, period. What makes you think Barbara Jean can get into college, or should? She's not just another David in black-face, you know. From what you've told me about her, she's a mixed-up schizophrenic kid who'll be lucky if she doesn't get knocked up or put in an institution."

"That's only part of it," said Molly. "She reads *Ulysses*."

He groaned. "That's exactly what I mean. What kind of pretentious nonsense is that? What can a sixteen-year-old kid get out of a book like *Ulysses?*"

It *does* mean something, she wanted to tell him. Barbara Jean's come farther in a few years than most people do in an entire lifetime, she's entitled to a chance, but it was hopeless. "I don't understand you any more," Molly said, instead.

But she did, of course. He had been isolated from life too long. He was so used to having everything under control in his work—and at home—that he could no longer abide deviation, or uncertainty. Instead of mellowing, he had grown rigid.

So she did not talk to him. She had realized that for many years now they talked only because she picked a topic. It was like being on a perpetual date. When she began dating Robert seriously, so to speak, she stopped trying to entertain Mike. She brought up the usual domestic matters—the plumbing at Quogue and David's telephoning or not telephoning (how many marriages, at that, could survive the absence of both maintenance and children?)—and Mike gave the appropriate responses. But he never initiated conversation. The result was that she lived in her own world,

Mike lived in his. So far as Molly could tell, he hadn't noticed any difference.

Certainly he appeared oblivious right now, as they sat in the apartment eating breakfast, presumably together, actually where? He was reading the second section of the *Times*, the first section on the table at his right, as usual. When he finished the second section, he would hand it over to her, and she would take it, with a faint flicker of resentment, also as usual. (The standard cartoon reaction. Yet why should *he* get the paper first? On the other hand, it certainly did not seem right for *her* to get the paper first. She had cited it once, humorously, as one of life's typically insoluble dilemmas, and Mike had pointed out that it wasn't. "You can always order two papers.")

She poured herself a second cup of coffee and remembered something she wanted to ask him. "Do you want to go out to the country Friday night or wait until Saturday morning? The Morses would like us to come to dinner Friday."

"I'm going to Washington Friday," he said. "I won't be back until Saturday night. No sense going to Quogue that late."

"I wish you had told me," she said tightly. She had arranged for the roof man to come over with his estimate Saturday morning.

"Edna must have. She had my schedule."

There was a message that Edna had called, Molly remembered. It was on her desk when she got back to the office in the afternoon, but she never returned the call. She didn't feel like it.

"I'm tired of having a secretary tell me when you will and will not be home," she exclaimed, and realized it was true. She was tired of it. It infuriated her.

"Well," said Mike calmly, "you were always complaining before that you couldn't make any plans."

"Why can't you tell me yourself?"

"Me?" He was surprised. "I have too many other things on my mind. I have my work to do. I can't be bothered keeping track of minutiae. That's Edna's job."

"It's all right for me," Molly said evenly. "My work is just busy work, occupational therapy. It doesn't matter if I get bogged down in trivia."

Without even indicating he had heard her, he put down his cup and began to push back his chair. Whereupon Molly exploded.

"That's typical of your whole attitude," she said. "Maybe my work isn't as important as yours, but it's important enough, and even if it wasn't, it wouldn't matter. The important thing is that it's important to me. But I'm always expected to turn off whatever I'm doing at the office as soon as I leave. I'm not supposed to work late. It's all right for you to be at the lab until all hours, to work Saturday and Sundays if it pleases you, but if I have to do anything after five o'clock, the world comes to an end."

He started to speak, but she overrode him. "You may not think you complain, but you do. You sulk. And besides, I manipulate so much that you probably aren't even aware when I'm late. Especially since you hardly ever come home when you say you're going to, anyhow."

"What is it you want me to do?" he asked when she stopped for breath. "Take charge of your social calendar?"

"That's not what I'm talking about."

"Well, what are you talking about? You sound irrational to me. I don't know what's come over you lately. It's impossible to live with you."

"Because for once I'm telling the truth?" She had not known the depth of her resentment until the abscess opened, and the pus poured out, hot, slimy, putrid. "*I'm* a second-class citizen in this house," she told him, loathing the way she sounded. She was turning into a whiner, worse than Julia, she thought, but she couldn't stop herself. "You think you treat me like an equal because you do me the great wonderful favor of letting me work. Who's kidding whom? We use my money, exactly as we use yours but at the same time we pretend it has no source. It's as if it drops from the trees. You can stay on the phone all night at home, checking with the lab, but if Angela calls just once, God forbid, I have to apologize and go into a great song and dance about what a pest she is. Our life revolves around your schedule, not mine. I thought it would be different when David wasn't here, but it isn't. It's exactly the same. You decide when you want to go on vacation, it's up to me to swing it. If it weren't for Angela . . ."

"Are you finished?" he said then, and stalked out of the room.

She followed him to the hall and watched him accusingly as he put on his raincoat.

"Goddammit, Molly," he said finally, glaring back, "you nag me so that I can never start a day with my mind clear. If this keeps up, I'm not coming home."

"Don't," she said, and he picked up his battered satchel and banged the door behind him.

She started to get ready to leave herself, and then remembered she had to strip their bed so that she could leave the laundry outside the door for the laundryman to pick up later in the morning.

She pulled off the top sheet, removed the case from her pillow and then, moving to Mike's side, yanked his pillowcase off. Then she pulled off the bottom sheet and tossed it angrily to the floor. You could do a Rorschach on the state of a marriage by watching a wife make a bed, Molly reflected. If she puts on the sheets carefully, pats a pillow, and hugs a pajama top to herself as she carried it gently to a closet, things are going well. But if she slams a bed together, she's unhappy in it.

As was she.

It had started soon after Robert came back from his ski trip. Sleeping with Mike became the adultery. For a while she had managed to conceal her turmoil when she and Mike went to bed. Buttons were pushed, response was elicited. She became a vending machine, selling herself. Once, when the machine seemed to

jam, she happened to think of Robert, and it worked
again. The next time she found herself unable to re-
spond, she made herself think of Robert, and then felt
so disgusted she got up and sat in the living room
reading until dawn. Meanwhile, slowly, inevitably, the
mechanism faltered. Last night, apparently, it had
broken down completely.

Mike had clearly made a gesture but she pretended
not to notice it, lying rigid on her back, arms crossed
and eyes closed, like a tomb effigy in an English chapel.
The man who married a numb wife, she thought to
herself despairingly, and the small witticism cheered
her so much that she became suffused with a pitying
affection for him and reached over to pat him. Unfortunately, as she did so, her brief surge of feeling
became grounded, and she turned to stone again as
Mike responded to the overture.

"I don't understand what's the matter," she told him
in a small voice. "I want to." She felt panic-stricken.
Was her body betraying her? Was it refusing to lie
any more? "Maybe in a little while . . ."

"It's all right," He was very gentle. "It happens. Just
relax."

Nothing helped. Her mind said: "Go ahead," but her
body screamed: "Rape!"

"Menopausal," he diagnosed finally, clinically, and
she heard a faint note of superiority in his voice. He
was only a year older than she was. "Don't worry. It
will pass. See if Arnold can give you something . . ."

He patted her shoulder kindly and turned his back to her.

Shaken, she didn't know whether to be pleased or enraged at his assumption. "You can't have it both ways," she told herself after a while. "Be glad you have an excuse."

But she had suddenly had the feeling her life was racing out of her control.

Sighing, she stuffed the linens into the laundry bag and, picking up her gloves and purse, walked toward the door.

She had to talk to someone. If she didn't, she would burst. Or tell Mike. She ached to tell Mike. She walked around with an inner hand clamped to her mouth to keep from telling him. She wanted to tell him when she was angry in order to get even with him, she wanted to tell him when he ignored her to puncture his unconcern, she wanted to tell him when she felt guilty so that he could punish her. But most of all, she admitted to herself, she wanted to tell Mike so that he would feel sorry for her. She wanted him to know how hard it was for her, how torn she was, how miserable and guilty and suicidal she felt. She wanted him, after his first understandable shock and disapproval, to tell her that what she had done was, after all, a very ordinary thing. She wanted him to comfort her, to absolve her, to make her understand—dear Lord, she wanted *him* to make her understand that she really had done no harm, not to any of them, and it was just something that happened. It would pass.

She was unbelievable, she thought then, beneath contempt. She decided to speak to her mother. She could not burden any of their friends with it, and shouldn't, even if she could, but her mother would not be upset. Her mother had no particular feeling for her, and she had never liked Mike, he never flattered her. Besides, her mother held her tongue.

Before she left, Molly checked her hair in the hall mirror and noticed some lines around her mouth. She had never seen them before. Were they there because she was frowning? She made her face a blank, but the lines remained, and she had the fleeting thought that she had better watch out, before long she was going to look old.

CHAPTER 9

When Molly called, her mother, surprised, had said, yes, she could be home a little after five. She was playing bridge, but she would leave early.

"Well, in that case," began Molly, already sorry she had asked, but her mother, point made, was now on the next play. "I really don't feel like bridge," she assured Molly quickly. "I'm just going because Kitty couldn't get a fourth."

It was a pity her mother had agreed to cut short the bridge because by the time five o'clock came, Molly was sorry that she had asked to see her, but under the circumstances, she couldn't cancel out.

It was disloyal to discuss anything to do with one's marriage with anyone else, she thought, taxiing over to

her mother's apartment hotel. It was unthinkable to
mention its sexual aspects. Did she really feel this way,
she wondered, startled. If so, how could she possibly
spend her life encouraging clients to "ventilate" their
problems? Was she a hypocrite? Did she use her skills
to trick them into self-betrayal, or was she being help-
ful? She pushed the questions into a closet of her mind,
and slammed the door. (Some other time, she thought,
not now.) On the other hand, in the face of the greater
disloyalty, wasn't she quibbling? Which was worse?
Being unfaithful, or talking about it?

The question reminded her of Norah Larson. Norah
had been Molly's supervisor when she did her field
work at Children's Aid. Norah had been married for a
short time only, too, but she was in her late thirties
and her husband, Allan, was considerably younger.
Norah worshipped him, and he seemed to love her
very much, too, but his eye continued to wander
nevertheless. He even called Molly one day. It was not
possible that Norah was unaware of this, but she never
gave any indication of being anything but overjoyed
at being married to Allan. Only once did she let slip
something that might have remotely referred to his
escapades, and Molly had never forgotten it. "Infi-
delity isn't important," Norah had said, apropos of
nothing at all. "What is unforgivable is the bad man-
ners that allow you to find out about it."

That was one way to look at it. Then Molly thought
of the young woman she had met at the Friedmans'
cocktail party some weeks before, and giggled.

A LOVING WIFE

❀

It was a big party, and Molly was alone for the moment, having detached herself from a group to get herself a drink, when the young woman appeared at her side. She was exceedingly attractive, all exposed bosom and massed red hair falling in Edwardian curls. She seemed to be drinking straight gin.

"Come talk to me," the young woman had implored. "Only I have to sit down." She collapsed on the steps nearby—the Friedmans had a duplex—and Molly leaned on the handrail. "I'm absolutely dead. We were horseback riding in Tarrytown all afternoon, and then I had to rush over to Romeo's when we got back to get my fall put on before they closed."

The young woman shook her head. "I can't keep up with him," she went on. She pointed to a tall, white-haired man at the far end of the living room. He had what Molly always thought of as a Helen Keller face—strong features with so much sensual expression that it was disquieting to look at him. "I'm his third wife. The first died and the other one divorced him. He was unfaithful to both of them. Me, too, now, probably," the young woman said reflectively, "but it doesn't matter. I'm crackers about him. He's marvelous in bed. Might as well share the wealth."

❀

The taxi pulled up in front of her mother's apartment hotel, just as Molly realized something curious about the way she had been thinking. In each case, it was the men who were unfaithful, not the women. Women were not supposed to be unfaithful. Was that, for God's sake, why she was suddenly compelled to talk to her mother? Was she looking for disapproval? (Or did she want to flaunt her conquest?)

Certainly her mother did not encourage confidences. She never had. When Molly was a child, her mother was either practicing the piano—before she married Molly's father, she had dreamed of being a concert pianist—or she was lying on her bed with the Venetian blinds closed and an icepack on her head. She suffered from migraines. When Molly ran in from school, her mother used to call out: "Just let me finish this section, and I'll be with you, dear," or the maid would say: "Sh, your mother's resting."

So Molly used to talk to her father.

When she told him she wanted to marry Mike (she had long before given up hope that Adam would ask her—she wasn't even sure where he was then, last she had heard he had been in North Africa) her father had asked her simply, "Do you think he's the one for you?"

"Yes," she had said. "I do. We have such a good time together. I like him so much. I can think of all kinds of reasons why we shouldn't get married, but still . . ."

"I don't believe in logic when it comes to making important decisions," her father had said. "Important decisions should be snap judgments."

Molly looked at him in amazement.

"'How do I love thee, let me count the ways,' all

nonsense. If you have to count," he said, "forget it. All
it has to do is add up to one."

It didn't—not quite—she had realized even then, but
she was afraid to admit it. Instead she exclaimed:
"That's one of my favorite poems."

"I know it," said her father. "Didn't I hear you when
you memorized it for class that time?" He had looked
at Molly very seriously. "Can you imagine not being
married to Mike?"

She felt a surge of relief. "No," she said honestly. "I
can't. I really can't. It just feels right for me."

"Fine," said her father. "Then it's right with me."

Did he really approve? She never knew. He must
have had some doubts because he came into her room
the night before the hastily arranged wedding and sat
on the edge of her bed. "You can't predict how a marriage is going to come out," he told her. "I've seen the
most story-book wedding end with the bride and groom
coming back and getting an annulment, and I've seen
marriages I wouldn't have given two cents for still be
love matches after twenty years." He patted her hand
and smiled. She had loved his smile. "Who would have
thought your mother would put up with me so long?
You should have seen her when she was your age. She
was even prettier than you, if that's possible. Beauty
and the beast—that's what we were!" He was not a
good-looking man, that was true. The first time Molly
came home from Wellesley, she had been surprised at
how short and round her father was. Until then, she

had thought he towered over her. He had died of leukemia while she was carrying the baby.

Her mother had moved to East Sixty-second Street. It was so convenient to everything, within walking distance (on fine days) of her hairdresser, her doctor, her dressmaker, and Carnegie Hall. (She always felt Leonard Bernstein had let her down when he allowed them to move the Philharmonic to the other side of the Park.) She spent the summer in the Adirondacks and part of the winter in Clearwater with her brother and sister-in-law. Every other spring, she went to Europe, by ship, and she was a patron of the Museum of Modern Art, although the most modern painting she owned was a Zorach watercolor Molly's father had picked up in Maine one year when they visited Molly at camp. Her mother, Molly had realized quite a while ago, was unquestionably the single most powerful influence in her life. Whenever she was in doubt about what to do, she tried to think of the action her mother would take, and then did just the opposite.

And yet here she was, going to her mother with her life in her hands. Melodramatic, but that was exactly how she felt. She was not going for punishment. That was a bit of cheap analysis. She wanted advice, and she would get it. Her mother was no fool; Molly knew it. She was not nearly as critical of her as she had been. If her mother had not changed her ways, she was at least consistent. She gave little quarter, and expected less. She expected nothing, as a matter of fact. She had her apartment, her way of living, her acquaintances, and she depended on no one who was not hired and paid to be leaned on.

In a way, Molly realized with a start, her mother was much more like David and his contemporaries than she was. She played it cool. She did as she pleased, like Queen Victoria taking it as her due that the chair should always be behind her when she wished to sit down. It was inconceivable that her mother should ever have lowered herself enough to take a lover. Or was it? What about Victoria and that Mr. Brown?

Not my mother, thought Molly, but the thought intrigued her as she walked toward the lobby. She nodded at the doorman—he had once told Molly he "adored" her mother, she was "such a real lady"—and took the elevator to the twelfth floor.

CHAPTER 10

She plunged in immediately, afraid that if she let her mother say anything at all, she would no longer be able to sustain the illusion that she might be able to help her.

Her mother heard her out without comment, sitting, straight-backed as always, in the little oyster-white bergère that had been her favorite chair ever since Molly could remember. She indicated neither compassion nor distaste.

"What it comes down to," Molly said, "is that I can't live with Mike any more."

Her mother frowned, and for a moment, Molly thought she was going to say something, but she didn't.

"And yet I don't want to leave. I can't do it to him. It wouldn't be fair." Fair to whom? To Mike? To herself? Or was she thinking mainly of Robert? "I can't announce out of thin air that I'm walking out. Nothing is any different. There isn't anything else I want to do anyhow. This thing with Robert—I know it's an aberration. One morning I'll wake up, and it will be finished, and I won't be able to understand how I ever got myself into it."

Her mother was shaking her head as if she thought Molly was holding something back.

"He really hasn't done anything," Molly said hurriedly, as usual quick to defend Mike from her mother. It was all right for her to complain about him, but she could not allow her mother to do so, she was too prejudiced. "Actually, in some ways he's much nicer than when I married him." It was true. If they were to meet now—free of the years that had passed—they might be able to have a very good marriage. The terms would be more equal. "He's certainly nicer than Robert. More my kind of person anyhow." In which case, what in God's name was she doing with Robert? It was a mystery.

"He won't marry you," her mother interrupted. Her voice was flat. "There's no point in your getting a divorce."

How could she be so sure, Molly thought angrily. Didn't she think it was possible for anyone to be in love with her? She had made a mistake in coming. "I don't want him to marry me. That's not the point at all."

Her mother reached behind Molly to the library table and extricated a cigarette from a small flowered

china box. It looked stale. "His kind never leave their
wives. They're unfaithful because they want to stay
married."

She could not understand why her mother was so
obtuse. "I'm not talking about his marriage. I'm talking
about mine."

"Don't do it," her mother insisted. Then, to Molly's
surprise, she had added: "It's no good being alone. I've
hated every minute of it.

"I guess I should have remarried," her mother went
on. "I could have, I suppose. I was almost as young as
you are, remember." Prettier, too, altogether more de-
sirable, her expression said.

She had been at least ten years older, Molly thought
suddenly, more likely eleven. Why did her mother have
this compulsion to put her down all the time? Did she
find *her* threatening? Did she try to figure out what
Molly would do every time she had a problem, and
then do the opposite? "Why didn't you?" asked Molly.

"Because I didn't want to go through all that again."

"All what?"

"Being married," her mother said delicately. "I had
Charles and you, and then I was through with it."

Her poor father. She had never thought of her
parents in sexual terms. You never did, unless someone
like Dr. Ziegler thrust your nose into it (therapeuti-
cally, of course), but the assumption was always there.
You existed, *ergo*. Her father was such a warm and
loving man, too. "What did he do about it?" She had

A LOVING WIFE

no right to ask, Molly supposed, but after all these years, what did it matter?

"You know what he did." Now her mother sounded irritated. "I admit it's foolish to go on being so upset about it after all these years, but I still resent the way you took his side without once thinking of how it was affecting me."

"I don't know what you mean," Molly said, puzzled.

"I tried not to show it, but there were times when I actually hated you. You'd totally ignore me, and then come back from Lucy's positively bubbling with 'Lucy, this' and 'Lucy, that . . .'"

"Aunt Lucy?" Molly was still bewildered. "You minded Aunt Lucy? Why?"

Her mother stared at her. Finally, after a long moment, she asked quietly: "Do you mean to tell me you didn't know Lucy was your father's mistress?"

Lucy was the widow of her father's first law partner. Their closest friend. A soft-spoken, plain woman with hair that had been white for as long as Molly could recall. She lived in Connecticut, in a small house on the Sound, right near the club where Molly's father played golf. Most Saturdays in the winter, when the course was covered with snow, her father would take her for a ride in one of the big cars he turned in every year and they would stop at Aunt Lucy's for a while. She always had wonderful toys for Molly to play with, and when Molly grew older, interesting books to read. She had died of cancer the year after Molly's father died. My God, Molly found herself thinking, could it really be

110

contagious? Mike had decided some time ago that it was a virus. It was not possible that those wonderful Saturday trips she took with her father were a fraud. He wouldn't have used her as an excuse to sleep with Lucy, would he? She thought of how she used to lie on her stomach in front of the fire, and read, and nibble the chicken corn Lucy kept on hand for her, and was suddenly chilled. "No," she told her mother carefully, "I didn't know it."

"You see," said her mother, "even in that, you take after him. You're exactly alike."

At last it was out in the open. She would have a chance to come to terms with her mother's hatred while she was still alive. She would not open a drawer one day while sorting out her mother's possessions, as had her old schoolfriend, Charlotte, and find a sealed letter addressed to her with the proviso: "To be opened in the event of my death." In most respects Charlotte's mother's letter was like any other maternal missive written on the eve of a departure for a thyroidectomy or a North Cape cruise. It contained instructions for the disposal of gold chains and diamond brooches and made an anguished attempt to shout across the void what had never been said loudly enough before. The only variation was in the message the writer wished to convey.

"What was mine is now yours, Charlotte," said the letter. "The trust sees to that. I am sure you are no more interested in any advice I may have to give you now than you were in the past. But I cannot let the occasion—myself, too, if you will forgive the jest—pass without letting you know, for the record, that I think you should have a bad conscience about the kind of daughter you have been to me. You have been headstrong and unfeeling, and I cannot truthfully say I have had any pleasure out of you since your infancy."

For months after she found it, Charlotte had carried a copy of the letter in her wallet, and showed it compulsively. "Isn't it fantastic," she would say, pink with amusement. "Did you ever hear of such a bitch?" When she showed it to Molly, it seemed to her that the words had been etched with fire, as if Charlotte's mother had picked them out with a child's wood-burning set. Molly had memorized the letter in that one reading, and now she saw why. Deep down, she had been afraid that was how her own mother felt about her, and now she saw that she had been right.

"We're not alike," Molly protested. "I can't manage an affair." Even as she spoke, Molly realized that she had not once questioned the truth of her mother's revelation, not even to herself. Quite obviously, it had not been a revelation at all.

"But you do."

"I don't." She wanted to smash every bibelot, every Baccarat paperweight, every Canton bowl and every Delft miniature in that stifling living room. "There's a lot more involved than my not wanting to be in the same house with him. I can't stand to be in the same room. The same bed. When he touches me, I have to keep myself from pushing him away. I can't

sleep with him any more. My body freezes up on me."
Was she shocking her mother? Tough. What did she
think it was all about anyhow? "I've been pretending
for months, but I can't any more." She paused for a
moment and then said bitterly: "I don't know how you
got away with it."

"Aren't you being a little melodramatic, Molly?" her
mother asked, ignoring the last. "You're not exactly
Anna Karenina. You're not the first woman to have an
affair, and you won't be the last."

"I know," said Molly, "but I feel like it. That's what's
so absurd. I sound like that serial you used to listen to
on the radio. 'Can a girl from a small mining town in
the West find happiness . . . ?' Something like that.
That's just what does worry me. Only I put it a little
differently. Does she have the *right* to expect happiness?
Is it wrong for her to go out and look for it?"

Her mother made a slight move toward her, and
then sat back in her chair. "I'm not sure it's wrong to
have an affair, Molly," she said, almost gently. "If two
people are unhappy together . . ."

"But we're not unhappy together," Molly protested
automatically, and then stopped short. "I don't think
it's wrong at all," she went on after a while. "But what
am I going to do with my monogamous body?" She
was one of the last Puritans, stumbling over sex, Molly
thought. People certainly weren't going to do that
much longer, were they? Love was love, and marriage
was marriage, and there was no longer anything that
said they had to go together, not even a song. "It's all

your fault," she told her mother with a sad smile. "I'm emancipated, but I still hear your footsteps outside my bedroom door."

"I should hope it would be your father's," her mother commented tartly, to Molly's pleased astonishment. "The trouble with you is," her mother added, "you keep trying to twist everything around until you can justify it. Some things aren't right, they're wrong. If you do them, you have to be prepared to take the consequences. I certainly never discussed Lucy with your father, but I don't suppose he thought what he was doing was right. He could have looked for excuses. I can't begin to tell you how many men I know who were doing exactly the same thing, flaunting their mistresses, some of them. But I'm sure your father felt he was doing wrong and that he was unhappy about it a good deal of the time."

"That's because he loved you." Why did she feel bereft, saying it?

"I know he did. I was the one. I didn't love him. That's probably—it's very hard to keep on loving someone who doesn't love you. I don't think you ever loved Mike either. I never did think so. You went off with Adam that time, and then he wouldn't have you, and you were scared to death you wouldn't get married because of the war, so you took Mike on the rebound. I told your father so at the time, but he wouldn't believe me. He was an incurable romantic, especially when it came to you."

Molly was speechless.

"I don't know if I am capable of loving anyone," her mother said wistfully.

"I wasn't sure I was either," said Molly. "I wanted to love Mike, and in some ways, I did. Do," she corrected hastily. "I do love him. But this thing—" she took a deep breath. "It tears me apart." She appealed to her mother. "Is that what love is? Or is it just sex?"

"Is there a difference?" Her mother seemed to hesitate for a moment and then she leaned toward Molly. "I did have a love affair once when I was a girl. Not what you mean by an affair," she added hastily, "but I used to think I would walk over burning sands to be with him. I don't know. I have an idea I was attracted by what I couldn't have. He was out for bigger game. All it added up to when you came down to it was a box of Huyler's candy and a corsage of tea roses."

"What shall I do?" Molly asked her, totally drained.

Her mother shrugged and retreated. "I don't know. It's hard for me to think of giving you any advice. You've always been the one with all the answers. You even bossed Charles around when you were children."

Because Charles never would take responsibility for anything, that's why, Molly wanted to say, but she refrained. If anyone was an incurable romantic, it was her mother, over Charles. Now that he lived in Pasadena, Pat, his wife, sent flowers east every Mother's Day and picked a present out of Gump's catalogue every Christmas, and her mother thought no more doting son existed.

There was no help for her here, Molly thought, and

rose to go. But before she could stop herself she burst into tears. Her mother, startled, put a tentative arm around her, and Molly pressed her knuckles against her nose, trying vainly to stop sobbing because she was getting tears all over her mother's immaculate beige silk dress. "Don't cry," her mother kept saying. "It's going to be all right, you'll see." She pushed her gently aside after a while, got a tissue from somewhere inside her dress, and wiped Molly's face. "Sit down," she said.

Molly did.

"I must tell you something," her mother began slowly. "I'm ashamed to admit it, but until this minute, I think I was glad you were having trouble. I think I've been jealous of you. Is that possible?"

They had looked at each other in silence for a while. Then her mother said: "Don't get a divorce unless you're sure of getting married again right away. Being divorced must be even worse than being a widow. At least, if you're a widow, you can't blame yourself."

"But I told you I can't . . ."

"Sit it out. It will pass. Everything does, except loneliness. For some reason, that gets worse. You wouldn't think so. You'd think you get used to it, but you don't. The older you get, the worse it is. Maybe because you give up hope of it ever being different. I used to think being married to your father was like being squeezed into a tight shoe," she said. "I thought the only way I'd ever be free again was if I got it off. But you can't walk without a shoe. Not where I go, anyhow. I'd have been glad to have him back long ago, even with Lucy. I'd settle for that."

"Do I have to settle? At my age?"

"At your age. You're a drug on the market. If you were a man, women would be stopping you and begging you to come to see them. I've seen it with my own eyes, right in my own elevator. There's a new man here in the building. He's about fifty, I guess, and apparently unattached. The women are around him like leeches. But there won't be any men stopping you. Not to marry you, certainly. I'm not saying you aren't attractive. You are. You've turned out to be really pretty. But you're still a drug on the market, Molly. And if by some miracle you do manage to get another husband, I doubt that he'll be any better than what you've got. Chances are he won't be. All the women I know who've remarried—widows and divorcées both —did it out of desperation. And did worse. Unless they were very rich and could snare someone else's husband. Otherwise, the men they got were old, or sick, or spoiled. Or fairies," she added after a moment. "I've seen that happen, too."

"You paint a charming picture."

"You asked me. I tell you, I may not like men, but I don't like women very much either. And that's all you see if you're alone. Other women. Your married friends call you at first and think they're doing you a favor. Then the wives get jealous. Or the husbands object to having a third wheel around. There's always that sticky business of who pays for what. Even if they can afford it, they feel put upon after a while, and yet they're too embarrassed to let you pay your own way. Finally, it gets so your married friends don't even call to see how you are because they're afraid they'll have to invite you, and they don't want to be put on the spot. Most of them disappear on you, until one day they wake up to find themselves in the same boat. Then they latch onto you in a hurry. They think you've made it, they've no way of knowing otherwise, and they figure maybe you can show them a way out. It's a very charming picture."

"You're a remarkable woman," said Molly, and she meant it. "But you really aren't sure I should settle for what I have, are you?"

Her mother shook her head. "No," she said, "I'm not. After all that, I'm not at all sure what you should do."

CHAPTER 11

But if her mother wasn't sure what she
should do, Molly was. She should end it, she had
decided by the time she let herself into her apartment.
Once she had shown it to her mother, the whole affair
had turned shoddy, like the dresses that used to look
so perfect in the store when she bought them and then
turned out to be so wildly unbecoming when she tried
them on again at home for her mother. She should stop
what she was doing, grab the first protruding branch
she could reach as she tumbled down the precipice,
and hang on until she got enough strength to climb
back to the ledge from which she had tumbled.

Mike was not coming home for dinner, and she was
too upset to eat. She sent Arletta home and went to
her desk to write a letter. The words poured out so

A LOVING WIFE

rapidly that some were illegible, and she had to stop
every once in a while to re-form them.

"At first," she wrote Robert, "I was so unwilling—
afraid, rather—to have an affair that I was actually glad
each time we left each other. I was relieved that I had
gotten away with it another time. Not very romantic,
but that's how it was.

"I don't mean that I didn't get any joy out of it. You
know I did. That's why I couldn't keep away from you,
no matter how much I wanted to. Every time you
called I wanted to say 'not this time,' but I couldn't. It's
the most exciting thing that ever happened to me. I
told you that once. I don't know if you believed me, but
it's so. Still, I don't think I loved you in the beginning. I
think I loved your wanting me more than I actually
loved you. Just as now I probably love wanting you
even more than I love you."

She looked at the last sentence dubiously for a while
and then crossed it out. He would not understand what
she meant, or if he did, she wasn't sure she wanted him
to. Besides it was so banal. Like something from the
Hit Parade, or whatever it was they called it nowa-
days.

"Essentially I was untouched," she continued, knowing, even as she wrote it, that it was not true. "We
went to bed, we left, we both knew it was an interlude.
The fact that we met and parted was a guarantee that
nothing would be disturbed.

"But suddenly it's different for me. I find our part-
ings unbearable. From the minute you walk through

120

the door, all I can think about is that you're going to leave soon. We lie in each other's arms, and instead of the ticking of my heart, I hear the ticking of the clock."

Corn, she thought desperately, pure corn, but it was exactly how she felt, and she had an almost physical need to tell him so.

"I wish that for once we could go to bed like ordinary people," she wrote. "Just go to bed, not make love—" It was a burden, sometimes, having to make love on demand, lover or no lover. "Four o'clock Tuesday afternoon" could turn out not to be what one had in mind after all when the time came. Or an aphrodisiac, she realized, roused just thinking about it. It could work both ways, couldn't it? She shuddered and continued. "Go to sleep, bump into each other as we turned, push each other away unaware, wake up cranky, reach for cigarettes, get up grudgingly, half-awake, hungry for coffee, not sex."

It would end it, she told herself, putting the pen down for a moment. That one night they had spent together when Jane was away didn't count. It was the only one they had had, and besides, she had been too frightened for it to have been commonplace—too frightened, and too happy. She picked up the pen again.

"Instead we have to leave each other just when we are most at one. We are wrenched apart. What is it the French say? 'To part is to die a little.' The moment I see you, I anticipate that little death. I am no longer happy when I see you. I feel bereaved."

She reread the last paragraph and shook her head. A lady in furs with violets at her throat. A lost lady, uncertain about the spelling of French clichés, forced to say it in English. She began to cross it all out and then slammed the pen down.

"Let it stay," she told herself. "Be exposed." For once, she vowed, she was not going to be a spectator at her own life. She was not going to perch on an analytical fence, eyes protected from the blinding sun by prescription sunglasses. It didn't matter if Robert was worth loving, it didn't even matter whether he loved her. She loved him. One way. No counting required, no logic in it at all.

If he so much as crooked his finger, she would come. If he nodded, she would give up Mike, David, her job, her friends, her safe house . . .

MAYBE.

For even as she slid down the cliff, she knew there was a net underneath, a trampoline that would toss her right back up again. She could throw herself at Robert because she knew he would not keep her. What she loved about him was his *not* wanting her. If once he really pursued her, if he ever in any way gave any indication whatsoever that he was playing for keeps, she knew exactly what she would do. Run.

"Try me," she thought then, "just try me. I surprised you this time, didn't I?" she told herself. "How can you ever be sure what I would do?"

She started to write again.

"So I think we had better end it before we get hurt."

Before she got more hurt than she was. "A relationship has to go somewhere. It can't stand still. Even a foot that falls asleep ends up feeling pins and needles. Since it can't end well, it's bound to end badly, in boredom or disappointment." Or betrayal, that was the real possibility, wasn't it? "Whatever it is, the end is going to spoil what came before, and knowing so pains me."

It reminded her of that other cliché, the one that was standard for funerals: "Our days are numbered." The last time she had heard it, at the funeral of an elderly aunt of Mike's she had never even met, she had had a fantasy of how it might be if it were literally true—if everyone went around with the number of his days inscribed on his forehead like a caste mark. Every day the number would change, just as that sign in Washington changed every time a baby was born in the United States. Only in this case it would be a matter of subtraction instead of addition. Could people possibly continue to be cruel to one another, to kill each other, even to be unkind, with that number writ in neon on each forehead? Click, click, cherish one another. Click, click—but it wouldn't work, Molly had decided. People would be so paralyzed at the realization of what was happening before their eyes that they would do nothing but stare into the mirror, or at each other. Imagine what it would be like for parents, or for lovers. Click, click, three more days to go. Or ten thousand. More likely, no one would see the numbers at all. They would turn out to be invisible, like the color of strangers' eyes. Only an occasional blue would startle.

"What else is there to say?" she wrote. "Just that I don't regret any of it. I never thought it would happen to me. Not *again*. At all." She should be grateful, she thought, but you had to be old to be grateful for the past. She should be old enough, but she wasn't. She had become vulnerable again, she thought. It was so easy to forget how it had been when you looked at the young. They seemed so remote, so self-contained, it was hard to realize that those hard shells were new, shielding bodies tremulous with longing, so freshly alive their skin had had no time to toughen.

She got up and walked to the window. Beyond the roof of the big, shadowed apartment house across the street she could see the last faint coral and magenta of the sun setting over the river, and she was twenty again, waiting vainly for a telephone to ring.

The young had no place to go these days, either.

Nothing could be planned, nothing could be permanent. It was the same thing, all over again. What was David going to do when finally he had to decide? Go to war, go to prison, go to Canada? Who could tell him what to do? They pitch their tents on the dark plain and make love with gunfire in their ears, she thought. Nothing had changed. She went back to the desk.

"The thing is I no longer have hope," she wrote then. "When you're young, at least you know that someday you will have a place, if not with this one, then with someone else. You may not want to admit it, but deep down, you know it's so. But this is it for me. In more ways than one it's an ending for me. I suppose one always thinks, 'Well, if it doesn't work out, I can always try again,' but now I have tried," she continued, sparing him no longer, "and it hasn't worked, and when I go back, it will be for good."

To the same place, she thought. Unless she was willing to move to a smaller place. Give up, cut down.

She put the pen back, folded the sheets of the letter together carefully, and then methodically tore them into bits.

Was it possible that she could decide to stay married just for the sake of things?

"I wrote you a letter," she told Robert idly, the next time they met. "One of my unsent letters. I tore it right up."

"Why?"

"Where would I send it?"

He sat down heavily. "You didn't have to send it," he told her after a while. "I know it by heart."

Of course he did, she thought, leaden. When bigger fools were made, they could use her as a model. "I guess you do," she said coldly.

He looked at her, puzzled at her tone, and then, understanding, became angry. "For Christ's sake, Molly!" he exploded.

She shrugged.

He took her hand. "I have a recurrent dream," he began, and then he stopped and grinned. "You know, you wouldn't have looked at me when I was twenty-five. I was the world's biggest jerk."

"I'll bet you were," she said, and smiled back. "Star-crossed, that's what we are. Hey," she said, knowing that the subject had to be changed, "do you know what I did this morning? I got your horoscope. I was waiting for the bus, and I saw an Aquarius one on the newsstand, so I bought it. I meant to bring it, but I left it at the office."

"What did it say?"

"It said you should sell short."

"I did," he told her. "Last week."

CHAPTER 12

The next time he had telephoned, Molly had hesitated, and before she had a chance to add "but maybe I can manage," as she had intended to, he said: "I understand. I'll call you another time," and hung up. With relief, it had seemed to her.

He had waited three weeks to call again. She sat out the interim very well. Like a robot, perhaps, but grateful, too, that it was being taken out of her hands. She had wanted it to be over, and now it was. He was not going to get in touch with her; if he did, she would hang up. It was the only way. Since there was no help for it, she thought, her mind echoing the sonnet she had said to herself over and over again that other time, so long ago, let them kiss and part. Or not kiss. But part. And all the while, sitting at her desk, grateful, her

127

hand drummed on the telephone receiver, itching to pick it up.

She was actually about to dial his number when at last he did call, and she was so startled that she told him.

"That's why I picked it up so fast," she explained, marveling.

"I missed you terribly," he said.

It didn't matter that she had told him. His cooling-off period, if that's what he had intended it to be, had worked. She was glad to hear his voice, it might be pleasant to see him, for old time's sake, and she would survive not seeing him perfectly well.

"I'd love to see you," she told him, all warm friendship. "One o'clock is fine."

When Robert walked into the restaurant, she didn't recognize him for a moment. Then she realized why. He had finally gotten his glasses. They were big, round, and horn-rimmed. The effect was enchanting. He looked like a mischievous small boy who had put on glasses for a joke.

"Congratulations," she said as he approached.

"Everything looms." He held out a hand in mock fear of falling. "I had no idea the world looks this way. I must have been walking around half blind for years."

"I'm sure I do. I keep reading the strangest things. Coming over just now I saw a bus that said 'Sex Ave.' The other day I read 'Pot Parties' for 'Patients' and I passed a 'Wizard' store."

"What was that?"

"A bar. The West End. What I like the best, though, is how I read something I jotted down myself—'Parallel lines meet at *infirmity*.'"

He ordered two martinis on the rocks, very dry, and double lamb chops. "That's marvelous. True, too." He looked at her over the glasses. "What made you write that?"

"Write what? Oh, about 'parallel lines'? I don't know. I was just doodling." She did know, and she decided to tell him. They had enough "No Trespassing" signs between them already. The moment of falsehood had long since gone. "I guess I was thinking about us," she told Robert, "Mike and me, I mean. We've gone along parallel for so long . . ."

"Infinity is a pretty long time to wait."

"Yes, it is," said Molly, warmed that he knew what she meant. She picked up her glass, took a gulp and put it down again. "I'm not sure I can go on, Robert."

The chops arrived, he cut into one and began eating, without stopping to look up from his plate. For a moment Molly wondered whether he had misunderstood. Then he put his knife and fork down and said slowly: "I don't know what to say to you," and she realized he had understood all too well and was frightened.

"You don't have to say anything to me," she said quickly. "It has nothing to do with you. Nothing at all." She had said too much.

"Anything that concerns you concerns me."

"Robert," she said firmly, "you don't owe me anything, and I don't owe you anything. We both got our money's worth." Or were both cheated. It amounted to the same thing. They were even. "There was something wrong in my marriage before I met you, else I wouldn't have seen you. You don't see a man unless you're looking for him. Not someone like me, anyhow." Was it true? Or was she just trying to make things easier for him? Molly Gilbert, binder-up of other people's wounds, while her own blood soaked into the rug, unstanched. "But I'm confused," she told him honestly. "I don't think I want to be married to Mike any more. I don't know what to do."

He took her hand, and Molly had the wild idea that he was going to tell her everything was going to be all right. They would start all over again, both of them together, and they would be happy. He would not hear of anything else. She tried to think how it would be, and all she could see was two long, straight lines stretching into a void, like a giant Op Art painting. She grew drowsy staring, until all she wanted to do was leave, walk away from that thick-carpeted, wood-paneled, hushed dining room and go home and go to sleep—forever.

"I wish we could be together," he was saying. "I'd give anything in the world for that." He spoke slowly, as if he had to force each word out.

She frowned but said nothing.

"I mean it." He picked up his knife and fork again and then slammed them down. "It hasn't been what I expected." He signaled the waiter. "Check, please. You don't want coffee, do you? Let's go."

She was light-headed with relief. She was free. When they reached the street, she murmured something about having to hurry back to the office and turned away from him, but he paid no attention and took her firmly by the elbow instead, steering her toward the Toledo. He handed her a key. "I'll be up soon," he said.

He must have picked up another key at the desk because he let himself in without knocking. He had tulips this time, red ones. She had an impulse to seize the flowers from him and break each scarlet head off, methodically, one by one, but she did not move from the armchair where she sat, coat still on and pocketbook in her lap. Without a word, he put the flowers on the dresser, walked over to her, put her pocketbook on the floor and carefully removed her coat. Then he sat on the edge of the bed, facing her, and took off his glasses. His eyes were bloodshot. "I care for you more than anyone else in the world," he said flatly, "and I will not leave Jane and my children."

The room was suddenly lighter, as if a cloud had moved away from the sun. He cared for her, Molly thought, he really did care for her. She straightened up in the chair and exhaled slowly. "I shouldn't have burdened you," she said.

"I didn't expect it to be this way."

What did he expect it to be like, she thought. She was a ping-pong ball, one moment happy, the next bitter. What did he think she was going to be? A quick roll in the hay? Like the others?

"I'm hurting you," he said, seeing her face. "What I mean is, I'm involved."

"You never were before."

"That's right. I never was."

"Congratulations. Or am I supposed to say I'm flattered? Okay, I am. I'm flattered."

"Please don't."

"Please don't what? I'm just following the script. It's very easy. The words go trippingly on my tongue. Now I say . . ."

"Stop it." He was very angry. "What the hell do you think you're doing?"

Molly crossed her arms over her breast and with her eyes closed, began swaying in pure terror. The next thing he was going to say was that it was no wonder she had made a mess of her marriage, compared to her, living with Jane was . . . She opened her eyes and found him smiling at her.

"Come on, Molly-o," he said, "don't pick a fight with me."

She submitted to being undressed and lay back passively. He took her abruptly and in her anguish and humiliation, she had one orgasm after another.

When she was dressed again, he made her sit down. "I want to talk to you, Molly."

"There's nothing to talk about."

"I'm a bad husband," he told her. "Constitutionally bad. I know it. You wouldn't put up with me."

"I don't want to," she said in a small voice.

"I wish you did." He rose. "Don't think I wouldn't like to have my cake and eat it too."

What else is there to do with cake, she thought, but eat it? Even if you freeze it, it has to be eaten sometime. It was an idiotic thing for him to say.

"I've thought about it, but it would be a disaster," he said.

They waited for the elevator together and when it came, he put her inside and pushed the down button. Then he waited for the elevator to come up again. Molly went to the lobby and walked through the revolving door alone, and as she did so, she realized something. He had not said he would call her. It was the first time they had ever parted without his saying he would call her.

He did not call the next day, nor the day after, nor the day after that. She stood it for a week, huddled in a dark cave with wings of panic brushing past her like swooping bats. Then, when she could stand it no longer, she called him.

It was midafternoon, and his secretary told her he was not expected back until five. "Who shall I say called?"

"Mrs. Gilbert," she said, boiling with sudden anger.

He still had not called back when she left finally, at six o'clock.

CHAPTER 13

When Molly got in before nine the next day, there was a message on her desk, but not from Robert, from Mrs. McGinnis.

Molly called her back immediately.

"Molly?" Mrs. McGinnis always shouted into the receiver as if she was afraid her voice might not reach faraway Manhattan. "They'll be calling you from the infirmary, but you never know when they'll get around to it. It's Barbara Jean. She went on a rampage last night. Put her fist through my living-room window."

"Oh, no."

"Right smack through the window. Smash." Mrs. McGinnis sounded as if she had enjoyed it. "I don't think it's too bad, though. They had to take stitches and the nurse told me they're getting some specialist in to look over the tendon. But I don't think it's too bad."

What was she going to do now, Molly thought. If she left and Robert called . . . "I don't know if I can get out," she began.

"Oh, I'm not saying you should come out," Mrs. McGinnis put in quickly. "I didn't call you for that. I just thought you'd want to know."

"What triggered it?"

"Beats me. She was my best girl lately. And then, whee, just like that . . ."

"I'll be out," said Molly, "this afternoon."

She went directly to the infirmary. Coming into the Oak Hollow grounds, trees in new leaf, dogwood about to blossom, and the earth soggy with promise, she had had a sense of *déjà vu* which was reinforced by her walk to the room the nurse on duty had pointed out. It was essentially the same corridor she had walked down at Bellevue nine months ago—bare, dismal, with flaking buff paint. The only difference was that this corridor was short.

She pushed open the door and there again, propped up in bed, was Barbara Jean. One hand was bandaged this time, instead of both wrists. She was holding a book in the good hand. As soon as she caught sight of Molly, she pushed the book under the sheet.

"Hi," said Molly.

Barbara Jean grunted. She had done something unpleasant to her hair. Streaked it with blonde dye. Maybe that's why she looked so different. Nine years, not nine months, older. What had they done to her here? Her obvious innocence, that incredible, inexplicable, undeserved (by anyone who dealt with her, Molly had thought the first time she became aware of it—no one really earned it) innocence was gone. Its loss was visible.

"What are you reading?"

"A book." Then, relenting: "About Malcolm."

"*The Autobiography of Malcolm X?* I just read it myself. I thought it was marvelous."

"It's okay."

Molly pulled up the one chair and sat down beside the bed. "Does the hand hurt?"

Barbara Jean's face quivered and for a moment she looked like her young self again. "A little. No, a lot." She leaned toward Molly. "It hurts a lot, Mrs. Gilbert."

"I'm awfully sorry," said Molly. She waited. "I wish you had called me," she said after a while.

"I didn't know I was going to do it," Barbara Jean told her. "I was sitting there in the corner, on the window seat, and the rest of them was fooling around, you know the way they do, dancing, wrestling, throwing pillows at each other, and all of a sudden, I couldn't take it no more. So I punched out the window."

"Did anything happen before that?"

For a second Barbara Jean's eyes widened. Then, almost as if she was afraid of saying any more, she put on The Look. Molly could almost see the mask being drawn down. Blank and contemptuous at the same time, The Look made its wearer impervious. It was impossible to tell whether the person behind it was angry, interested, hostile, bored, or terrified. Molly understood why it was put on, but The Look always outraged her. It seemed to her she was seeing it more and more lately. On case aides, handymen, elevator operators, salesgirls, even on Arletta's face. They shouldn't be doing it to her, Molly thought. She had done nothing to them.

"Won't you tell me what's troubling you?"

The Look varied a shade to admit a faint touch of amazement. "Who said anything's troubling me?"

"Something must have set you off," Molly persisted, knowing she shouldn't. "How can I help you if I don't know?"

"I dunno."

Molly pushed back her chair and tried one last tack. "Did you have a fight with your mother when she came Sunday?"

Barbara Jean shook her head.

It was hopeless. It was one thing to be understanding; it was another to permit oneself to be abused. It was no kindness for her to sit here and add to Barbara Jean's guilt by allowing her to behave this way. Molly got up, said good-bye, and left.

She was going out the infirmary door when she realized what must have happened. She turned around, walked back down the corridor, went into Barbara Jean's room and looked at her sternly. "Didn't your mother come to see you Sunday?" The project, she knew, had finally sent Julia train tickets and money for a sitter. Her caseworker had been reporting for months that Julia was anxious to visit Barbara Jean, but where was she going to get the fare? Take it from her food allowance? Or the rent money?

Barbara Jean said nothing.

"I asked you," Molly repeated, "did your mother come to see you Sunday?"

"Her?" asked Barbara Jean coolly. "Who wants that cunt to come?"

All Molly could think of on the long ride back on the Long Island Rail Road was how much she would like to smash her fist through a pane of glass.

When she got to Pennsylvania Station, she called the office.

"No," reported Beth, "no messages at all, Mrs. Gilbert."

CHAPTER 14

Essex Street this beautiful spring morning looked like a city struck by plague. There was nothing alive in sight, not even a stray cat. The children, Molly knew, were all inside, if they were not of school age, sometimes even if they were. They had no shoes, and if they had shoes, they had no jackets, and if by some miracle, they had both shoes and jackets at the same time, the doorways and cellars reeked with danger. Even Molly felt it as she walked toward Julia's house. There were few house numbers on Essex Street, so the taxi driver had let her off a block too soon. The houses there had been boarded up, their organs so diseased and sclerotic that they were no longer able to sustain even the minimal life the Department of Welfare was willing to subsidize. The disease seemed to be spreading, too. It was approaching the corner house where Barbara Jean's mother lived on the second floor. It was only a matter of time before it took over that house, too. They ought to start looking for a place for Julia now, Molly thought automatically, not wait until they would have to take anything, out of desperation.

She went into the vestibule and pushed Julia's doorbell, knowing as she did so that it probably did not work. It had two names on it—Oglethorpe and Washington. Washington was Barbara Jean's name. She was the daughter of Julia's original husband, the one back in North Carolina. "We're first families," Barbara Jean had said once. No ironies were ever lost on her. After Molly had waited a decent interval, she pushed open the vestibule door, stepped in and then almost retreated. She could see two shadowy figures on the floor, half-entwined, half-leaning against the balustrade. Two men, or a man and a woman, she couldn't make out which and didn't wait to try, but hurried up the steps. Apparently they had not noticed her. She wanted to get away before they did. Distracted by seeing them, she had forgotten to close off her nose and breathe through her mouth, as she usually did, coming into a hallway down here, so the smell assaulted her—that sickening distillation of urine, wine dregs, rat fur, rancid grease, dust, and the fermented hay fumes of pot. There was no smell of cooking here, as in the tenements of Mulberry Street and Chatham Square. No one cooked on Essex Street any more. They ate TV dinners or opened cans. Before long the children here would act like the children of Apulia when they were given their first hot meals by CARE. "They cried," her Italian social worker friend, Cassandra, had told Molly once. "They actually cried out in terror when they felt the heat on their tongues."

The door at the head of the first landing was ajar. The wall next to it bore a sticker proclaiming, "Johnson has bad trips." Where did that come from, Molly wondered. "Mrs. Oglethorpe?" she called. "Julia?" Molly tried, but she could never get out the Oglethorpe more than once. It was too ridiculous a name. It sounded like a put-on.

"I'm here," called Julia. "Come in and slam the door behind you, Mrs. Gilbert. Them kids is always leaving it open."

The bathroom was just inside the door, its door ajar, too, and Molly was pleased to see a douche bag hanging over the shower rail. The kitchen came next. It seemed to have been newly painted, a stark white, and it had a travel poster saying "COME BACK TO EIRE" scotch-taped to the wall. As usual, by dint of effort Molly was not sure she would have been capable of, it was immaculate.

The next room, though—the living room, ostensibly, although it served as a bedroom, too—looked as if it had been through a riot. It was strewn with mattresses, cartons, run-down shoes, a grayish bundle that might have been rolled-up sheets, a faded red satin ribbon with "SUCCESS" inscribed on it in tinsel, and a large black rubber boot with a gash across the toe. A set of bunk beds stood in the middle of the room, and Julia was sitting calmly on the edge of the lower one, a pink sock pulled tightly around her head. The four younger children were playing in the debris around her feet. Except for the oldest child—Edmund, Molly thought it was—none of the children had any pants on.

"Sit down," said Julia. "Anywhere. Just push that stuff on the floor." Molly cleared the oilcloth-covered hassock Julia was pointing to and sat down. "We had another flood," Julia continued. "I'm letting everything dry out good. Last time I put them away too soon, and everything got mildewed."

"I was wondering," said Molly.

"Those mothers in the hall bother you coming up? Edmund said they're out there again. Mostly they're just sniffing glue, but sometimes . . ."

"No," said Molly, "they didn't bother me. They didn't see me."

They looked at each other warily for a while and then Julia said, "Go ahead. Say it. I did it again."

She must be at least six months pregnant, Molly had thought. "That's why you didn't go to see Barbara Jean?"

Julia nodded.

"I figured it must be something." Molly had been on her way to see the new drug addict counseling service the Center had just set up in an East Village loft when she had decided to stop off and see Julia first. "I checked with the project," Molly told her, "and they told me this time they really did give you the carfare."

"I'll give you back the money," said Julia.

"Oh, for God's sake," said Molly, furious with her, "that's not why I came. Did they call you from Oak Hollow?"

"No," said Julia warily. "Why? Is anything wrong?"

They should have called, Molly thought, angry with Oak Hollow now, and then she realized they couldn't have, even if anyone had thought of calling Barbara Jean's mother. They wouldn't know Julia had a telephone; it was a secret, and the number was unlisted. A telephone was one of the many items *verboten* to Julia, even more frowned upon than men, probably. It cost money. Of course, in the long run, Molly reflected, men also . . . "Yes," said Molly. "She broke a window and cut her hand."

"Oh sweet Lord Jesus," said Julia, "not again!"

"She's all right. I saw her on Tuesday."

"I know I should go out to see her, but I'll tell you the truth, I don't want her to see me this way."

That was a new reaction, Molly thought, with some surprise.

"I promised her," said Julia, "no more kids. There's too many of them as is." She patted Edmund on his head and poked him gently. "What you hanging around my legs for? Go in the other room and look at TV. You still got it on." He did not stir, and she turned to Molly again. "The doctor told me I got to make

Barbara Jean feel happier. Well, I'll tell you the truth, seeing me now wouldn't make her feel happier."

"Didn't they give you the pill?"

"Can't take it. Don't you remember my varicose veins? You can't take pills, you got varicose veins, you get a stroke. I can't take those other things either, that diaphragm or that loop they try to talk you into. I can't take them on account of my kidneys. I have something else. Like shaving cream it is. It works pretty good."

"So I see."

Julia guffawed. "Buster came over with a couple of quarts of beer, and there I was." Then she became serious. "It wasn't no accident. I knew what I was doing. I'm sorry about it now. It wasn't good judgment, I see that now. But I tell you, all of a sudden, I got such a hankering for a baby. I needed one so bad . . . you know how it is?"

Molly closed her eyes involuntarily for a second and then opened them quickly. "I've only got David. I told you about him." It was a *non sequitur*. Nonprofessional. So was the next thing she found herself saying. "I had a woman come in for counseling a few months ago who told me she wouldn't sleep with her husband any night except Thursday. Do you know why?"

Julia shook her head.

"Friday was the day she changed the bottom sheet."

Julia laughed again till the tears rolled down her cheeks. "You must be kidding."

"No," said Molly, "I'm not."

"Well," said Julia soberly, "she sure must have a hard life."

"She does."

The children were now exploding. The two middle children—girls—had put the youngest, a boy who had to be about two, Molly thought, although he was very small for his age, in one of the cartons, and he was crying to get out. Edmund tried to stuff a shirt into his mouth to stop him from crying, the carton tipped over, and the girls began to jump up and down yelling, "Mama, Mama, look at Edmund!" Julia got up quickly and cuffed all of them except the baby, whose tears she wiped off with the palm of her hand. "Now you get out of here," she said firmly. The three older children fled, and Julia went back to the bunk bed, with the baby on her hip. She set him on the bed and there he remained, motionless, for the rest of the time Molly was there.

"What am I going to do about Barbara Jean?" Julia asked then.

Answer the questioner, not the question, thought Molly. "I guess you miss her too," she said.

"She's the only friend I got in the world," said Julia simply. "I wish she was back."

"I'm sure you do."

"When she's not here, I'm like a person that's setting down thinking. The only relief I get is locking the kids in and going out on the street and walking. I walk and I walk, and then I turn around and come back." She shook her head sorrowfully. "I know this is no place for her. She's better off where she is."

Molly thought of the yellow streaks in Barbara Jean's hair. "I'm not so sure," she said.

"She's a smart kid," said Julia. "They're going to help her in that school. You told me so yourself." She stopped and looked at Molly curiously, as if, for the first time she realized what Molly had said, and was puzzled.

"She's very smart. She was coming along very well . . ." Molly stopped. She couldn't say anything. Like a mouse in a maze, her mind searched for an opening, something that made enough sense for her to be able to say it aloud, but she could find nothing. She had no answers any more. Not for anyone. As she realized what she was thinking, she corrected herself automatically. She was no longer able to help anyone look for his *own* answer, she told herself, but changing the words made no difference. She was still helpless.

"I don't want her to be like me," said Julia. "I don't want her to have this life. I don't want her to be loused up with no kids. I want her to get out of here."

"You should call her up," Molly said flatly.

"I can't. If I talk to her, she'll find out. I can't keep nothing from her. I'm not ready for her to know—not yet."

Maybe it would go away, Molly thought bitterly. That was a good way to handle a problem, turn your belly on it and then maybe it would go away. "Why don't you write her a letter?" she suggested, with barely concealed hostility.

"That's just what I was going to do," Julia said eagerly. "I started to write her a letter. Wait, I'll get it."

She went into the room where the children apparently were watching television quietly and returned with a ruled sheet of paper that looked as if it had been torn from a school notebook. There were a few lines written on it in pencil. "I'll read it to you," said Julia. "It starts: 'Dear Daughter.' Then it says: 'Excuse me for not coming to see you. I feel real bad about it. I miss you real bad. Every day I go out and walk but my troubles still torment me. It's like the Harpies and the Blind Man. My troubles follow me down the street wherever I go. I am the Blind Man and they are the Harpies.' That's all I wrote so far."

"That's very beautiful," said Molly. She blew her nose. "What made you think of Harpies?"

"I saw it on the TV. There's this program the kids watch. The lady tells very interesting stories sometimes. The Harpies is like big, black birds, you know, only they got women's faces."

"I remember now."

"Do you think she'll understand what I'm saying?" asked Julia.

"I don't know," Molly told her. "I hope so. I do. I think you should send it. Finish it up and send it."

"Okay," said Julia, "I will."

147

"Well," said Molly, "I guess I'd better be going." She stood up.

"Wait a minute." Julia went to the other room and called Edmund. "Put on your sneakers and come over here. This minute." She turned to Molly. "Let Edmund walk a ways with you. Till you find a taxi."

"Why?" protested Molly. "I'm perfectly all right."

"You're better off with Edmund," said Julia. "You listen to me." She touched Molly's sleeve lightly. "Take care of yourself, Mrs. Gilbert, you hear now?"

CHAPTER 15

The Center's new East Village branch
for drug abusers (as contrasted with "users"; it was a
nice distinction, Molly thought, walking the four flights
to the flat where the drug project was housed) looked
like Julia's place. Only it was not quite as neat, and the
posters were either orange and psychedelic or idolized
portraits of Ché Guevara. There was no one there except Bill Shields, the young director Angela had hired
fresh out of Hunter. He had apparently rushed to the
door as soon as he heard her step, and it seemed to
Molly his face fell when he saw who it was, but he
made up for it by greeting her warmly and giving her
a mug of coffee before she had time to catch her
breath.

"No doughnuts?" she asked.

"Sure," he said quickly. "I'll get you some."

"I was only kidding." She felt vaguely uneasy. Did it have to look like a pad?

"We must have food around," Bill explained earnestly. "That's half the problem with our kids. They never eat." He had on a Nehru jacket, jeans, soiled sneakers, and a gilded medallion hanging from a heavy silver chain. Working clothes, obviously. He was also growing a mustache.

Robert must come down and see how the place looked now, Molly thought. He would be delighted with what Bill had done, if only because no one else on the board would be. She had urged Angela to ask Robert to be on the committee planning the "secret" branch (it bore no identification and Bill was told to assume any role that seemed appropriate), and it was a good thing she had. Not only was Robert's interest so piqued by the undertaking that he had offered to pay the first year's rent on the flat but, more important, his involvement in the project had come at a fortunate time. It was helping to assuage his disillusion over the recent Oak Hollow garbage-bag imbroglio.

Recalling it now, Molly could not help smiling. He had been so outraged.

It was ridiculous, she acknowledged. Cottage parents were supposed to see that all trash deposited in garbage cans was put in bags first. One cottage persistently failed to do so, and the maintenance man assigned to it finally refused to empty its cans. The cottage father and the maintenance man had a few words on the subject, the maintenance man declared himself insulted and punched the cottage father, Sandy suspended the maintenance man, and the entire nonprofessional staff, child-care workers included, promptly staged a wildcat strike.

"How can they do it?" Robert had stormed, deeply affronted. It was less than six months since he had singlehandedly persuaded the board to ignore Ralph Low's objections to signing a contract under duress, and he was expecting an "I told you so" as soon as the Center president got back from his cruise on the *France*. "It's immoral," he told Molly.

She shrugged.

"Why didn't they take it to the grievance committee instead of walking out like that?"

"It was a matter of dignity, I suppose."

"Dignity," he repeated, "what about the dignity of honoring a contract?"

"Or," she said idly, "maybe they want more money."

"More money? But they're already getting . . ." He looked at her, startled himself at what he was about to say, and she laughed in his face.

"It's hard to take, isn't it?" she said. "But that's what it's all about—undeserving poor, ungrateful workers, deceitful children. Otherwise it could be a cinch."

It was just another toy for him, a new toy, like his Cypriot figurines, or his paddle tennis court, she had thought then, her chest suddenly constricted, and what she meant to him was . . . but she did not have the heart to finish the sentence, even to herself.

The walkout had ended with restoration of the *status quo ante* in all respects but one—the purchasing department provided plastic liners for the refuse cans, thus obviating any necessity for individual garbage bags.

But the episode had shaken Robert. The end of innocence, Molly reflected. It was a good thing the Center had some potheads to offer him, if, indeed, it could flush any out.

"Anyone turn up yet?" she asked Bill Shields now, somewhat eagerly. Everyone involved in setting up the project had agreed that prospective clients were not to be sought out. They would have to come of their own accord, if they were to be helped at all.

"Just one couple," Bill told her. "Last night. They had no place to sleep so I let them stay. They just left. It's a beginning. They'll pass the word around and then . . ."

It would turn into a flophouse. "Are you sure you should let anyone sleep here?" she asked dubiously.

"Why not? If a place to sleep is what they need? That's what we're here for, isn't it? To help?"

"I suppose so." It was all very confusing. Fortunately none of this was her responsibility. She had just come down because she had to get out of the office. She could not bear being there, holding her breath every time the telephone rang. "But you don't want to turn it into just another place to get a fix, do you?"

"It's a risk," he agreed equably. "But we agreed to take it, didn't we? It's the only possible way. Even Mr.

Singer said so. We can't tell them what to do. All we can do is be here, available, for whatever it is they want of us."

"Don't make speeches to me, young man," she wanted to say. "I've made them all myself." But he was right, of course. All they could do was stand by and try to break falls—and hope they didn't get an arm smashed in the process themselves. She stared at Bill's medallion. It looked familiar, but what was it? Siva, of course, that's what it was. Siva, the god who balances on one toe, destroying in order to create. She was extinct here, too, Molly thought with a pang, gone with Florence Nightingale, Helen Hull, Karen Horney, and the Philadelphia School of Social Work, dodos all. They had become as pertinent as drinking fountains for horses, she decided. Bill Shields, too, probably, only he didn't know it yet.

She departed as suddenly as she had arrived, aware that she had puzzled Bill, but unable and unwilling to do anything about it.

She returned uptown and went to Bloomingdale's instead of back to the office, wandering aimlessly from floor to floor until her head ached with frustration. When she got back to the first floor, she stopped to watch a dapper young man give a make-up demonstration. At the moment, he was painting an elderly woman's eyelids an iridescent yellow. Molly herself never used eye make-up. She couldn't keep it on. Whatever she put on top of her eyes was sure to end up either in them or under them, since she always seemed to be either laughing or crying or blinking away cinders. Maybe he could suggest an appropriate eyeshadow, though, Molly thought. That might stay put.

She peered into the mirror on the nearest cosmetic counter and decided against approaching him. She looked so haggard she was ashamed to face a saleswoman, let alone a young man. Shopping always threw her into disarray, anyway. It was an endless multiple-choice quiz for which she never seemed to come prepared. It was inconceivable that anyone would shop out of anything less than direst need. Incomprehensible that any woman could actually enjoy it. She made a last telephone call to Beth and went home.

After dinner, Mike had looked at her curiously and asked her if she felt all right.

"Why?" That was unlike him.

"I don't know," he said. "You seem a little strange."

"No," she said, "I'm fine."

"Oh." He picked up the *Post*, sat down in his leather armchair, and opened the newspaper at the center fold.

But a faint flicker of something—Molly didn't quite know what—had surfaced and she said tentatively: "Mike," and then did not go on. After a moment, she repeated, a little louder, "Mike?"

He looked up.

"There is something the matter with me," she had

said. "I don't know what it is. I feel as if I'm going to explode."

"Why?"

"I don't know. I'm exhausted, for one thing. I'm so tired I feel like bursting into tears all the time."

"That's what I meant. You've sure as hell been jumpy lately."

"I guess so."

"Probably working too hard. Don't break your neck so at the office."

Maybe she was breaking her neck at home, she thought, irritated. Did he ever consider that? She saw that he was glancing down at the paper in his lap and hurried to keep the conversation going.

"I don't think it's the work. I think it's something more basic. A kind of free-floating discontent. I don't think I'm accomplishing anything any more," she told him hopefully.

"Who is?" he said.

"Oh, it's different with you. It's right there in front of you. You know what you're doing. You see the results."

"I do?"

This time she heard him. "Of course you do." She hesitated for an instant. "You told me so once yourself —in science, even failure is an achievement. You find out what doesn't work."

"That's so," he agreed.

"If we fail, we hurt people. We can't afford failure."

"Why don't you look for another job?"

But that wasn't the point. She was both angry and disappointed. That wasn't her point at all. "I wasn't talking about the Center particularly. I was talking about social work in general. If anything, we're more relevant than most. We have this drug project . . ."

"Stay home," he said. "Take a vacation. Sometimes I wish I could quit for a while myself."

"You don't care if I leave my job? It doesn't make any difference to you if I work or not?"

"Of course not," he told her amiably. He picked up the newspaper.

"Aren't you interested in anything I do?" she asked, for the first time shrill.

Apparently he didn't hear her.

"Mike," she exclaimed, "will you put that paper down? You started this, I didn't. You asked me what was the matter with me. Let's talk about it."

He looked at her, completely bewildered. "What is there to talk about? I told you what to do. If you don't like your job, leave it."

"Just like that," she said. "Pick up and walk out."

"Well?"

"Nothing I do has any significance, does it? Suppose I told you to quit every time you said you felt bogged down? How would you feel?"

"Here we go again." He slammed the paper on the floor. "It's impossible to say anything to you any more. What do you want from me? You tell me you're not satisfied with your job. I tell you to leave it. You're lucky. You can walk out anytime you please. But if you don't want to, don't. What is there to discuss?"

"But it's not that simple." She was drowning, crying for help. Why couldn't he hear her? Or, hearing, answer?

"Look, Molly," he said, "I'm beat. Exhausted. I've had a rough day, too. Let's not get into another fruitless discussion about whether you should work or not work. I'm just not up to it."

"It's not my working I'm talking about," she said desperately. "That's ancient history. I've settled that in my own mind. You're always bringing up old scores."

"I thought I made it clear to you long ago how I feel about your having a job," he told her, ignoring what she had said. "I don't give a damn one way or the other and I'm not going to let you try to make me feel guilty about it."

"I'm not trying . . ."

"You do it all the time. You may not realize it, but you do. In very subtle ways. For instance, any time anyone mentions what I do, you're sure to point out the sacrifices I—and by implication, you—have made. You don't come right out with it, but the implication is perfectly clear. If it wasn't for your working, I wouldn't have been able to do it."

Well, she thought stubbornly, it's true, you wouldn't have been able to stay in that tower, but she said nothing.

"The fact is we don't need what you make, and we never did. I've always done damn well. Maybe," he

157

conceded, "not as well as if I'd gone into business, like Sam Ross, but that's something else again. You wouldn't have liked that either. But any time you were willing to stay home, you could have. We didn't need your money."

"How can you say that?" She was truly appalled.

"Because it's so. Actually a lot of times it would have been much better for me if you hadn't been working. I don't mean only your breast-beating about whether you were being fair to David, or the office, or God knows what. We could have gotten away more. I could have taken that year in Kyoto."

"Did I stop you?" she interrupted. "Didn't I tell you I'd take a leave of absence if you wanted to go?"

"Yes, after making it clear how hard it was going to be, the Center was changing its whole program just then, wasn't that it? And then there was David, he was just starting high school, maybe it was a bad time."

"It's unbelievable," Molly said. "No matter what it is, it always ends up exactly the same way. You weren't sure whether you wanted to go. You told me yourself they were way behind what you were doing, the question was whether you wanted to give up the time just for the sake of having a sabbatical in Japan." She was so angry now she was on the verge of bursting into tears. "You think you're giving me freedom, leaving all the decisions up to me, but you're not. You're just getting out from under. Talk about subtlety. You put on a great show of being the head of the house, but you always hedge. In the end, it's up to me, and if things don't work out, I get the blame. It's always been that way," she said, "whether I worked or didn't work, whether we lived in the city or the country, whether we had children . . ."

"What do you mean by that?" Mike asked.

She had surprised herself. "Just that. Did you ever tell me you wanted more children?"

"Tell you I wanted more children?" He was incredulous. "How could I? Wasn't *that* up to you?"

"It was up to me," she repeated. "That's exactly what I'm saying. It made no difference to you whether we had children or not."

"Of course it made a difference," he said. "But you were the one who had to have it. If you didn't want to go through it again—after what happened—I certainly wasn't going to force you."

"But you never even brought it up," she told him. "You never even mentioned it." Or held my hand and told me it would be all right, you would take care of me, nothing bad would happen to me, she thought, anguished. You never once told me to have courage, you would be there.

"Because it wasn't up to me," he insisted. "It was up to you. Whatever you wanted to do about it was all right with me."

"You see," she pointed out bitterly, "even in that, in a matter of life and death, you're still refusing to take responsibility, pushing it all on me. If you had only once asked me to have another baby . . ."

He stood up and punched his left fist into the palm

of his right hand. "It must be involutional," he said
finally. "It's early, but it's the only explanation."

"Brilliant," Molly said, "absolutely brilliant. But
you're wrong. There's nothing like that the matter with
me."

"There has to be," he said flatly. "I've never seen
anyone change the way you have lately. You used to be
a fairly reasonable human being. Now you're a god-
damned drag. It isn't possible to say anything to you
without your blowing up. I can't stand being in the
same house with you any more."

"But that's how I am. I'm not reasonable. I'm all
mixed up. I always have been." It was true, she realized, she had been skating on thin ice all the time,
doing figure-eights a hairline above the flood. "Why do
I have to consider your peace of mind all the time?
How about mine?"

"I haven't noticed you paying any great attention
to my peace of mind, but if that's what you think
you've been doing, you can stop it. Right now. Just
take care of yourself. Don't interfere with my life, and
I won't interfere with yours."

"But I want to be interfered with. That's what I'm
trying to tell you. I want more interference, not less. I
want you to care about what I do." Nora trying to get
back into the doll house, Molly thought. That's what
she sounded like. But who knew better how cold it
was outside?

Mike shook his head helplessly. "I don't understand
you at all."

"Why not? You spend your whole life trying to figure out what makes things tick—why can't you devote a little of that brilliant mind of yours to studying me?"

"Cut it out, Molly," he said then. "Understand? You cut it out."

She glared at him.

"You're getting close to the edge, Molly," he went on. "I told you before, I've had it. Don't push me. I have my problems, you have yours. I don't burden you with mine. I don't want to be burdened with yours."

"But that's what marriage is, Mike. We're not roommates, we're not friends, we're husband and wife. We should be held together by something more than crisis —or minutiae. By now we should be a single whole, open with each other, able to say anything and everything to each other . . ."

"No one says anything and everything to anyone else. You want to say everything that comes into your head, go see a psychiatrist. You'll never know whether he listens or not."

"That's contemptible," she said, heartsick, but she made a last effort. "Mike, what I'm trying to say is that we should listen to each other more. Me, too. Maybe I don't listen to you enough either. It's bad enough to be lonely if you're not married," she pointed out, "but to be lonely *and* married . . ."

"What have I been doing for the past half hour except listening to you?" he asked helplessly.

"That wasn't listening. You've just started to listen."

Her face crumpled. "Oh, you'll listen to me now. You always do if I scream loud enough, if I explain what I want to say and why it's important, and force you up against the wall. But you want to know something? By that time, I don't need you to listen to me any more. I don't even want you to listen. I've talked it out with myself."

"All right," he said. "You're finished? Now let me tell you something. You think living with you is any picnic? You think just because you take care of unimportant housekeeping details, you carry your share of our marriage? Well, you can think again. I don't need you for a housekeeper. I can hire one. I can have my meals out. I won't have to keep looking at the lab clock because, God forbid, Arletta's already put the chops on. I can take my own shirts to the laundry, and maybe I can have some peace when I come home. Because I'm getting damned tired of walking on eggshells." He picked up the paper, and then, impulsively, dropped it again. "One more thing. You want to say anything you please? Fine. But I reserve the right to say what I think about what you say."

Now it was her turn. "I don't understand you."

"I know you don't. Not," he added hastily, "that I want to be understood. I'm just trying to say that if you insist on my listening, I'm going to express an opinion."

"Of course."

"No 'of course' about it. I found out a long time ago that you don't want honest answers. You want approval. Well, I can't do it. Either I say what I think, or I don't say anything. That way I don't get my head taken off."

He didn't really like her, Molly realized, seeing his expression, any more than she liked him. It was a sobering thought.

"You know, you're not always right," he added curtly.

"It has nothing to do with right or wrong," she pleaded. "I'm not talking about who's right and who's wrong. Why can't you get that into your head? I'm not talking about judgments. I'm talking about communication. I don't want comments from you, either way. All I want is an ear."

"I told you," he said, "if you want an ear, get yourself a Viennese psychiatrist. Tell him to go 'hmm.' But get off my back."

He was impossible. "All I want from you is a little human sympathy," she persisted. "I want to be able to say I'm tired without you telling me not to break my neck at the office or quit. Just once, I'd like you to say, 'I'm sorry you're tired.' That's all. Just that. 'I'm sorry.'"

"But suppose I don't feel that way? Do I have to censor every word I say to you?"

"No, but I don't want to censor every word I say about myself, either. Not about *you*. Myself. I don't want to invade your privacy, just mine."

"I'm sorry," he said, "I'm not a *voyeur*. I'm not comfortable watching someone else masturbate."

That was the night she moved into David's room.

❀

They managed to avoid each other for the greater part of the week.

On Friday morning Mike asked if she wanted to go out to the country, and she replied that she preferred not to. There was a conference she really ought to attend on Saturday.

"Okay," said Mike. "Then I'll go out myself."

"Fine," she said.

He hesitated in the doorway for a moment, went out, and came right back again.

"Maybe you'd better do some thinking," he said, "about what we're going to do."

"What do you mean?" she asked, panicked.

"I've been doing a lot of thinking," he said, "these past few days. I thought we had a pretty good life. You did what you wanted to do, I did what I wanted to do, we brought up a good kid. I thought we had it made. Now you tell me you've been put upon. I don't understand you . . ."

"You don't."

"I know. I've neglected you. I don't call you at the office to chat, or send you flowers. I forget anniversaries. The whole bit."

"It's always a cliché. Until it happens to you."

"That's right. Until it happens to you." He was tight-lipped. "I've faced up to a few things myself, too. First of all, *I've* had it. I'm not going to make it." He gave a harsh little laugh. "I'm not going to get a Nobel Prize, Molly. Not even a Lasker. It's not entirely my fault.

164

Some of it's bad luck. I just happened to go down a
track that didn't pan out. If I had picked viruses instead of steroids . . ." He shrugged. "Well, I didn't,
and that's that. I do a sound job, I've got good people
with me, I make my contribution. But there isn't going
to be any big payoff. It's too late."

"Nothing's too late," she said, shocked, but she knew
better. You did it young in research, or you didn't do
it at all. Mike said so himself, long ago. What was that
anecdote he always told his students? Something about
Einstein telling Eddington he had done only a half
hour of creative work in his whole life, the rest had
been commentary? And did Eddington reply that he
himself had worked only ten minutes—or was it five?
She couldn't remember. But she did know why the
anecdote stuck in her mind. She had always assumed
that Mike was going to have at least a minute or two,
eventually.

"Everything's too late," he told her. "I don't kid myself, Molly. But I won't downgrade myself, and I'm
not going to let you do it either."

"But I don't. I admire you."

"For what I'm going to be, Molly," he said, "not for
what I am."

She could only stare at him, her jaw slack.

"Well," he said then, "I've got to go. As I said, you
think about it. You decide where we're going to go
from here. Anything you decide is okay with me."

He was out of the door before she could pull herself
together enough to say anything.

It was like seeing a house on the edge of a bluff collapse into its own basement, leaving a tangle of exposed wires, old furniture, shattered plumbing, family pictures, and torn strips of gay wallpaper.

And it was all her fault.

She had pushed it down. Blindly.

None of it was Mike's fault. He hadn't changed. He was the same as always. No more selfish, no more single-track, no more cavalier than before. And no less kind, or honorable.

She flinched. Then, reflecting, she made herself admit that he shared the blame. It was bad enough as it was, she didn't have to slash herself, too. Why hadn't he told her? Why did he have to wait until now, until all they had in common was rubble? She was no magician. How was she supposed to know what was going on in his mind if he didn't tell her?

That was when the full enormity of what had happened to her struck her.

She should have known. That was her stock in trade. She was omniscient. Strangers opened their hearts to her. Children sought her out when she came into a room. She was a gifted caseworker, wasn't that what her supervisors always used to write on her evaluations?

She buried her face in her hands and wept. She was a fraud. In every sense. That was why their quarrels had been so corrosive, salting instead of cleansing. Because she was dishonest. They had had an open house, and she had smuggled betrayal into it.

CHAPTER 16

She felt like a lemming, Molly thought, racing helplessly toward the sea.

Everything she touched seemed to go wrong. Doors slammed on her fingers, zippers stuck, Beth failed to appear for a few days and never called to say why. She made no headway with clients—as a matter of fact, she seemed to sense an antagonism on their part she had never noticed before. She couldn't stand her friends, and Angela was more pettish than ever.

Molly knew what it was, of course. Robert. Not because it was over. She wanted it to be over, God knows, not for anything would she have started again. But it was unfinished. She could not bear loose ends. Uncertainty. She needed to write a period before she went on to the next sentence.

A LOVING WIFE

She telephoned him, and Robert said, yes, of course he would see her on Wednesday, as she had suggested, he had been meaning to call her himself, he wanted to see her very much. He would let her know where in a day or so. As soon as she hung up, she made an appointment to have her hair washed and set. It seemed essential that she approach that final meeting immaculately. For some reason, she had thought of her grandmother and pins, then, and smiled to herself. Her grandmother had lived with them briefly and Molly remembered very little about her, but her adjuration about safety pins had made a lasting impression. "You must never put a pin in a petticoat, Molly," she used to say, "or in anything else you wear. Supposing you were run over and got taken to the hospital; wouldn't you be ashamed?" It was years before Molly realized that if she got run over, one pin more or less would hardly make a difference. Still, she never used a pin.

She was on her way to the hairdresser now. She looked at her watch. She had left the office too early. It was another half hour before she was due. Just as well. She would have time to stop at Bonwit's and get some slips. All the ones she had were suddenly much too long. She went into the store, bought two very expensive short lace-trimmed petticoats and then took the elevator up to the fifth floor instead of going down. The B. H. Wragge section sometimes had nice clothes, she recalled. She looked through the size 10 rack and pulled out an understated pale-blue wool that would be just right for . . . and then, for the first time realiz-

ing what had been in her mind, put it back quickly and
hurried to the elevator.

She arrived at the hairdresser's a quarter of an hour
late, which meant she now had to wait while Mr. Anthony did a comb-out. Someone apparently had left a
copy of *The Nation* in the midst of the *Harper's Bazaar*s and *House Beautiful*s. It was an old one, so Molly
thumbed through it quickly until she got to the PER-
SONALS on the last page. They were not as interesting
as they used to be, she thought, or was it the *Saturday
Review* that had the fascinating ones? This one
seemed to specialize in advertisements for car-bumper
strips—"Incest Begins at Home," "Melt General Her-
shey"—that kind of thing. Not very distinguished. Also,
announcements of computerized matchmaking. "Let
TEAM make you a team," said one. No fee named.
"Searching? It's not enough to just 'know thyself.'
COM/PAIR, the 'people-matching-people' of Princeton,
speeds your research." That one cost ten dollars. Reasonable enough for an alter ego, thought Molly. She
put down *The Nation* and turned instead to the astrol-
ogy column in *Harper's Bazaar*.

But before she had a chance to read Pisces, she found
herself listening to Mr. Anthony's comb-out, a black-
haired young woman in slacks and T-shirt, who was
quite obviously beside herself with excitement.

"Oh, I never invite anyone I'm dating to a party like
that," she was telling Mr. Anthony. "It would spoil
the whole thing. I'd have to pay attention to him."

"How many are you having?" asked Mr. Anthony.

His hobby was cooking. Molly and he had exchanged many recipes over the years. His roommate, Mr. Tom, who manned the chair next to Mr. Anthony, loved to clean. "So it works out very nicely," Mr. Anthony had told Molly.

"About fifty. I got a bartender to help me handle them. The trouble is I have too many men. A man I used to go with who's married now gave me the names, and they run the gamut. You know, advertising executives, lawyers, doctors, accountants. I hated to leave any out, so now I don't have enough girls."

"What ages do you need?"

"Well, the men run from about thirty-seven to fifty. The girls are in the thirties. I'm the oldest really, but then I'm a once-married, divorced, you know, so it doesn't matter as much. I need more girls in their thirties."

"I'll ask around," said Mr. Anthony. "I have a couple of girls coming in later might be interested."

"They better not be dogs, though, you know. About eight o'clock. That's when I told the other girls to come. Gives us time to set out the food."

"What are you having?"

"Sicilian pizza. I cut it up in little pieces. Bite-size. Ritz crackers and cheese. Peanuts. Nothing sweet. I find a crowd like that doesn't go for sweets."

Mr. Anthony teased the last section, the dark lady besought him not to spare the hair spray, she had a hard night ahead of her, and then it was Molly's turn.

"What in the world was that about?" she asked Mr.

Anthony. It couldn't possibly be what it sounded like.

"What do you mean? Oh, the party." He shrugged. "She has them all the time. For singles, you know."

Molly shook her head.

"You pay a couple of bucks, have a beer or a Manhattan, maybe pick up somebody. I don't go for them myself, but it's not bad. It's a way of blowing an evening."

Enough of signs and portents, thought Molly. It was a good thing she never did get to find out what Pisces had in store for her. Life was alarming enough as it was. "What would you think of my having a rinse?" she asked Mr. Anthony idly.

"I've been telling you," he said, "a little bit of Loving Care, and you'd knock off five years just like that."

"Does it wash out?" she asked dubiously.

"Like a pair of stockings."

"Fine," she said. "But just a little." While he went for the right bottle, she made her usual inspection of the Clairol and L'Oréal diplomas Mr. Anthony had earned and noticed a new one. "DISASTER COLORIST" it proclaimed. Impossible. She bent a little closer. That was better. It said: "MASTER COLORIST."

When she got back to the office Robert called and said he was tied up for lunch but he could meet her at three o'clock, in the Village. He was borrowing an apartment from a friend who lived on West Eighth Street. Very sensitive on his part not to have them meet anywhere they had met before, or was it calculating?

Either way, it was immaterial. She was past worrying about that kind of thing any more.

Their rendezvous began very well indeed. She refrained from calling attention to the unbroken brown of her hair even when he gave her a friendly kiss and told her she looked smashing.

They chatted about the Center and what they had been doing since they last met, and then Molly looked at him cheerfully and said: "It's finished. Isn't it marvelous?"

"Not the feeling," he said quickly.

"The feeling, too," she told him with a smile. "I'll be honest with you. It really took me a little longer than it took you, but I'm fine now. I guess every affair has a life of its own, doesn't it?"

"I suppose so," he said dubiously.

"I mean," she said brightly, trying desperately not to reach out and touch him, "having an affair is like having sex. It's like ontogeny—an affair recapitulates sex. Men and women peak differently. It's more diffuse for women. It takes them longer to get started, and longer to come down when they do get started, but once women are down, they're down. Just like men. When an affair is over, it's over. Dead." She smiled at him. "We're dead, Robert," she said. "That is, as far as . . ." and her voice trailed off as it did when she spoke to Mike.

Robert looked at her without saying anything, and it was the same expression he had had that first time when she had stood, key shaking in her hand, in front of the door on the ninth floor at the Toledo. "Mrs. Gilbert," his face said again, "the efficient Mrs. Gilbert." The only difference was that it was then that he had probably begun to love her a little, and now he was becoming aware that he did not love her at all. Symmetry, she thought, oh, fearful symmetry.

"Ontogeny," he told her with considerable exasperation, "is what happens before birth, not after."

And what has this been, she started to say angrily, if not stillborn, and the pain in her gut gnawed so that she had to take a deep breath and could not speak.

"You're not very scientific," he went on, quite seriously, totally unaware of her agony. What he was going to say had obviously been on his mind for some time. "Do you say things like that to clients? You know, exaggerate so, make inaccurate generalizations . . ." He was floundering now.

"All the time," she told him airily. "It doesn't matter what I tell them, as long as I tell them something. You know that. Because," she said coldly, suddenly under control again, "they don't listen to the words, they listen to my heart. Angela says that, and it sounds like crap, but you know what? It's true. So is that other bromide of hers, 'Don't answer the question, answer the questioner.'"

"I didn't mean . . ."

She drew herself up very straight. "Let me tell you something else. I'm a good social worker, Robert. Not gifted like Angela, but very, very good. You don't know it—you don't know the first thing about social work, you just play at it. All of you board people do. You have no idea what it's really all about—any more than I can possibly imagine what you do downtown." She was safe, at last. Her office had been waiting for her all the time, four-cornered, rectangular, silent, hollow. "It's funny, isn't it," she said now, gently, almost affectionately, "how different people are in private—or maybe what I really mean is public—life. When they're doing their thing. You see a doctor socially, and he's boisterous, or egocentric, or so bland he melts into the woodwork. You can't imagine how anyone would even trust him to treat a dog. Then you have to see him professionally, and suddenly that same man is serene, modest, sure. His very touch makes you relax. He knows what he's doing, and you know he knows." She paused for a moment. "Even Dr. Ziegler—we kid about him—"

"Old *Zeitgeist?*"

She nodded. "Unbelievable. A horror. But put him in a room with a couple of squabbling parents and their miserable kids, and what he does with them—*for* them, I should say—is not to be believed, either. He's a genius."

"So he says." Robert smiled ruefully. "It's true of everyone, though—carpenters, auto mechanics, cello players, artists, even stockbrokers. You've either got it or you haven't, and it's obvious immediately. You're absolutely right. I wasn't putting you down, Molly-o."

"I know you weren't."

In the end, she went into the kitchen of the borrowed apartment and made coffee. They drank it companionably, sitting on the settee near the balcony overlooking the garden of the ground-floor apartment underneath. It was a pebble garden mostly, but there were two flower boxes against the far wall, filled now with yellow tulips a day or two short of opening. After an early start, spring seemed to be standing still this year.

They were thinking of building a house in Vermont, Robert told her. At Stratton, for skiing. "The kids want to go all the time," he said. "I don't mind the skiing, but I hate being in hotels."

"You do?" She raised an eyebrow, and he laughed.

"Unless I'm in good company," he amended.

After that, they were silent for a while. Molly tried to think of something to say, but all that came to her mind was how she had bought a new slip for this meeting. She yearned to make an amusing story of it, and the dress she had almost bought, without realizing that she had been flirting with seduction, how all the while lecturing herself that if she said so much as one word on the subject, if she tried in any way to be endearing, or naïve, or vulnerable, if she did anything whatsoever to try to woo him back, she would cut out her tongue. Personally.

"I think I'm going to take a few weeks off," she said finally. It was the first she had thought of it, but at least the remark was a safe one. Or was it? "Marion actually called me from England last week to remind me that I promised to visit her this summer."

A LOVING WIFE

"That would be great." He was really enthusiastic about the idea. "Where does she live?"

"Surrey."

"Be sure you go to Cornwall. It's magnificent. Wild, unspoiled."

And very romantic, she thought, all those potions and lovers. "I was thinking of the Hebrides. I've always wanted to go to the Hebrides. The outer ones."

"Mike going?" he ventured.

"If he can get away. He's up to his ears in work." Important work, she wanted to add, work that may save lives someday. "Maybe he'll join me later."

Eventually they left. Robert double-locked the door and put the two keys in his pocket so automatically that it struck Molly that the apartment might not be borrowed at all, but his. Or he stays there, she thought. I should have looked in the bedroom closet when I made the coffee. In which case, how could he have brought her there? She shook her head as if to dislodge something unpleasant crawling at the back of her neck.

"You going uptown?" asked Robert. "I'll get you a cab."

"Don't bother. I'll walk a little bit. It's so nice out."

"I'll walk with you."

At West Twelfth Street, Molly decided she'd better get back. Robert put up a hand for a cab. Molly stopped, patted his other hand warmly and looked him full in the face.

176

"Do you know what Richard J. Needham of the Toronto *Globe and Mail* says?"

"No," said Robert, "I do not know what Richard J. Needham of the Toronto *Globe and Mail* says."

"I read it in a magazine at the check-out counter in the market the other day," said Molly. "He says that 'inside every woman of forty-five a great love affair is screaming to be let out.' I beat me to the punch, didn't I?" She gave him a winsome smile. "I'm grateful, Robert, I really am."

"Bitch," he said, and since a taxicab halted in front of them at just that moment, it was the last thing she heard him say.

CHAPTER 17

Her humiliation was overwhelming.
She had been tried, and found wanting; discarded;
dumped. It was not possible that it had happened to
her; nothing like that ever happened to Molly Gilbert.
But it had happened, and she barricaded herself in her
office and hid out at home, ashamed to be seen with
the scar of rejection so livid upon her.

She had been sacked, thrown over, shown the door,
she told herself relentlessly; all she had left to hold
onto was the thin, lacerating wire of her own honesty.
Maybe if she said it often enough, she would get used
to it. It was not, after all, the end of the world. Besides
she was not being honest with herself. It had happened
before. She had survived then. She would survive
again.

Doggedly, desperately, she kept explaining it to herself. Nothing grows in a vacuum; everything has to be rooted in something, even an affair. She wanted to be loved for what she was; he wanted to be loved for what he did. They both got what they wanted, or at least gave each other the illusion of what they wanted. For a while. He made her feel lovable; she let him feel important. If the idea made her squirm, tough.

And having talked herself into sanity, she would sit at her desk and pound her thighs with her fists like a child in a tantrum. She could feel the anger rising in her throat and expanding in her head like a genie out of a lamp, until her temples ached with the pressure. She would cup her face in her hands, pressing her fingertips tight against the pain in her forehead, and ask herself: What? What now? What could she possibly do?

All she could think of was running away, but every road she came to ended in a *cul-de-sac*. She didn't want to stay with Mike, but she wasn't sure she wanted a divorce. Or if he did. Maybe, she thought, not daring to believe it, maybe he really did want a divorce. She had unmade her bed; maybe she wasn't going to be able to make it again. (Not even to lie in it, she told herself quickly, trying to take refuge in the pun.) She wasn't sure of anything. Not one single thing. She found her job unbearable, but she wasn't able to do anything else. She hated to be with people, but she feared for herself alone. She disliked New York, and she had nowhere else to go. It was impossible for her to come to a decision about anything—for the present, anyhow. That much she knew. The most she could expect of herself—and even that was more than she seemed capable of at the moment—was to float, fingers crossed against the engulfing wave.

It was Robert who had shoved her into the water finally, if unwittingly. He did it by running into Angela at a Center finance committee meeting and asking her whether Molly had left for England yet.

"What's this about your going to England?" she asked Molly when she got back to the office.

"What do you mean?"

Angela explained.

Molly had completely forgotten what she had said to Robert that last time. "Oh," she said then, "what a memory he must have!" Was Angela looking at her oddly, or was it just her imagination? "I think I know where he got it. Mike and I met them at the theater, weeks ago, and she said something about going to England, and I said something innocuous about wishing I could go, too." She regarded Angela warily. "Actually my cousin Marion has been begging me to visit her for years."

"It would do you good to get away," Angela said immediately. "Anywhere at all. You've been looking exhausted lately."

"I am," said Molly, suddenly limp with self-pity, "very."

At lunchtime Monday, on impulse, she walked over to Fifth Avenue, looked for an airline office, and bought herself an excursion-flight ticket to Rome. "You're lucky," commented the clerk. "We just got a few cancellations."

"Why?" asked Molly, before she remembered. The war, of course. For a few days it had even taken her attention away from herself. "It's all right to go, isn't it? Now that it's over?"

"It was all right before," said the clerk. "What difference does it make what happens in Israel? But some people . . ." He shrugged.

Her passport still had a couple of years to go, and so did her vaccination certificate, she was sure. She went back to the office to tell Angela she was taking her advice. "I'd like to start my vacation Thursday night. I can get everything on my desk cleared up by then. Is that okay with you?"

Angela looked as if she wanted to tell her something, and then seemed to change her mind. "Sure," she said. "I think that's fine, Molly. Just leave me a list of what you want me to take care of while you're away."

She was equally casual telling Mike. "I've decided to go to Italy for a few weeks."

"If that's what you want to do," he replied.

"I'll have to leave this Thursday to get the excursion rate."

"Fine." He walked toward the study.

She followed behind him uncertainly, waiting—for what? For him to stop her? Beg her not to go? "As you said, I need a change."

He fingered some papers on his desk. "I take it," he

said after a while, "I'm free to make my own plans, then."

She turned on her heel and left without answering.

He did not bring up the subject again until breakfast the next day. "I presume you intend to think things over," he said.

It was getting to be his favorite phrase. "I wish you would be more precise," she said. "What things exactly do you have in mind?"

He ignored the question. "You'll let me know what you decide."

She wanted to strike him. "Of course," she said stiffly.

"Thank you." He reached over her for the percolator and poured an inch of coffee into his cup.

"It makes no difference to you, either way?"

"Not much," he said, "frankly. Not any more."

"I'm glad," she told him. "That makes it much easier, doesn't it?"

"Uh-huh."

He did not come home until after she was asleep that night.

On Wednesday he had returned at about eleven o'clock. She was already in bed, reading. She heard him getting undressed but instead of remaining in the bedroom, he walked over to David's room. He had stood in the doorway for a moment looking at her, and then without a word, stalked in.

Torn between anger and pity, she had said nothing

when he got into bed beside her and switched off the light, and then she lay unresisting.

Afterwards he had gone back to their bedroom by himself.

She did not see him the next morning nor had she heard from him before she left the office for the airport. Alone.

And so they had parted in anger.

It was too bad, she told herself now, rechecking her seat belt. She should have made a gesture. She should have done something to make it easier for him. This way, if anything should happen to her . . .

Her grandmother's safety pin, she thought, trying to reach under the plane seat for her canvas carryall. What possible difference would it make whether they had said good-bye politely, or not at all, if the plane crashed and she was killed?

The plane landed then, so smoothly she didn't even feel the wheels bump.

Made it, she thought, suddenly light-headed with relief, and gathered up her things.

Since she had a seat in the back, she was one of the first out. The afternoon air felt tropical after the cold blast of the plane's air-conditioning. She paused on the tarmac for a moment, basking in the heat, then looked automatically up to the observation balcony to see if there was anyone there to meet her. The balcony was jammed with people—stocky old women with kerchiefs on their heads and newspaper-wrapped parcels in their hands; stolid old men with handlebar mustaches; young couples, frantic with pride, holding up infants stuffed into knit suits like sausages; solitary smiling men in shiny silk suits carrying bouquets; a young woman leaning over the railing, squinting anxiously. Everyone expected someone, and as always, arriving unannounced and unawaited in a strange place, Molly felt a pang of disappointment.

But this time it was even worse. No one waited for her anywhere.

CHAPTER 18

The airport seemed to be very far from the city. Naturally, they had landed at the new one. Last time she had arrived at Rome, she and Mike were coming from Dubrovnik and they had landed at the old one, Ciampino. The plane they were on then didn't need any jet strip. It had taken off from a cow pasture.

It was much better coming into Rome from Ciampino, Molly thought. You drove along the Appian Way, Respighi echoing from the dark pines, and by the time you got to the Forum, you were hearing trumpet voluntaries and the clash of cymbals. Arriving from this direction was like driving to Manhattan from Kennedy. Queens, Italian-style. Even the afternoon traffic looked the same.

Then her cab driver made a sharp turn and darted

down an alley, and Molly saw that she was wrong. It was Rome; she had been right to come. Brown and amber weathered houses huddled around a small, Romanesque church with a deer head on its steeple, and from the antlers of the deer there rose a jaunty cross. The driver slammed his brakes on a few yards past the church. Before she realized what he was doing, he had muttered *"Scusi,"* and vanished through the beaded portière of a small shop. He was gone for quite a while. When he returned, he was holding a small package by a string loop. "Okay," he said, with a reassuring smile, *"Uno minuto, Signora!"*

That was why it was taking so long. He had gone out of the way to pick up his package. It didn't matter, and even if it did, Molly didn't know enough Italian to make an issue of it. Besides, she told herself as the streets suddenly began to look familiar, they would be at the Luna any minute, just as he had said. But the episode bothered her because she knew perfectly well the driver wouldn't have done it if Mike were along —or if she were a man.

She was staying at the Luna. They always stayed there. It was a smallish hotel overlooking the Borghese Gardens and she liked to think that it was not a place where tourists went, especially American ones. When the taxi pulled up, she was pleased to see that the Luna had not changed at all. It even had the same doorman who greeted her warmly, as if he actually remembered her, and guided her by the elbow into the nondescript lobby.

186

A LOVING WIFE

The dark-haired young man at Reception was new, though. He spoke English with a German accent. "Nice to be back," Molly said valiantly, trying to make it clear at the outset that she had been there before, accompanied, but he only grunted. Last time, Reception had been ebullient, sandy-haired, and plump, with a family who kept an inn at Frascati. She and Mike went there for lunch one day, and his mother gave them a basket of figs to take back to Rome for him.

"Does Madame require a tub?" Reception inquired. "Or will a shower be sufficient?" His tone was scornful.

"I suppose so," said Molly dubiously, but he was obviously not interested in her answer because an even more dapper dark-haired young man was already at her side, holding a big black key embedded in a heavy brass disk. "This way, if you please, Madame." He was German, too.

She followed him past the reception desk into an inner lobby, puzzled because she thought the elevators were on the other side. He led her to a single old-fashioned, glass-enclosed cage elevator which took them to the third floor. There they walked the length of a corridor to an alcove with a door wedged into a corner before which a porter in a brown-and-white-striped apron waited with her suitcase and coat. The assistant turned the iron key briskly in the lock, threw open the door with a grand gesture, and motioned her in. "If you please," he said.

The room was gloomy even with the lights on. The wallpaper and the matching chintz draperies and bed-

187

spreads were dun-colored, with an all-over pattern of tiny, shrunken flowers that seemed to exude a musty smell. The assistant snapped on the lights in a closet that turned out to be the bathroom and beckoned to Molly. "I have seen a bathroom before," she wanted to say, but she peered in obediently. There was a stall shower, a basin, and a toilet. No bidet. Well, she wouldn't need one, she thought and then corrected herself. That was *not* what a bidet was for, and she knew it. She smiled, a little sadly, and went to the window. At least she could look at the Gardens. But there was no view. There was construction across the way.

She was more hurt than angry. "They'll be hammering in the morning."

"Oh, no, Madame," the assistant assured her. "Tomorrow is Saturday. No one works on Saturday."

"Don't you have another room?"

He shrugged. "I am sorry, Madame. It is the same everywhere. No room. The city is full. This is our last single."

Before she could say anything else, he had backed out of the room. The porter lingered, smiling apologetically, until she realized why. Then, contrite, she reached into her purse and handed him some coins. He pocketed them, unsmiling, and left abruptly, leaving her to wonder exactly what she had given him. She thought it was 200 lira. But maybe she had given him two 50-lira coins by mistake.

It was about time that she learned about money. It

was absurd to act like a retarded child every time she
was confronted with a check. Holding out a handful of
coins for waiters and cab drivers to help themselves
was not charming, it was irresponsible. "You must stop
putting yourself at people's mercy," she told herself
harshly. "It's not fair to take advantage of them that
way."

She pulled the chintz spread off one of the beds.
There were two beds, even though the assistant had
made such a point of its being a single room. A single
obviously was only a room they wouldn't dare offer a
couple. She lay down and felt better immediately. The
Luna's linen, at least, was as she remembered it—
heavy, starched, faintly damp, as if it had just been
ironed dry. It was like a soothing compress against her
tired body.

But she could not rest. She looked across the shabby
room to the bare dresser and longed for the flowers
that weren't there, the flowers that had softened the
ugliness of every rented bedroom they had shared,
and her loneliness was so intense it was like a stitch
in her side.

She jumped up. Time enough to sleep tomorrow.

She showered quickly. Even if there was no bidet,
the shower was good. It had a tiny faucet at the bottom so that the temperature of the water could be
tested with a toe before it was turned on full. She put
on a printed silk shift she had shortened for a second
time the night before she left, and examined herself

in the mirror. She was relieved to see that her hair
had survived the trip, too.

By the time she got to the lobby, though, she was
sure her slip was showing. Her mouth felt stiff, as if she
had just had a tooth filled under novocaine. She could
not make up her mind whether to smile as she walked
past Reception (woman of the world? innocent
abroad?) or appear distracted (so much to do? a
secret sorrow?). She decided to look stern. Let them
repent them of their chintz and their airshaft. When
she got outside, the doorman said "Good evening" at
the exact moment she said *"Buona sera,"* they both
smiled, and she told him no taxi, she was going to
walk, thank you.

The problem was in which direction. By now, it was
nearly seven. If she went to the Via Veneto, she could
sit at an outdoor café, but she might have to have
more than one drink before it would be late enough
to go to a restaurant. It would be better to go toward
the Spanish Steps first. She could look for gloves in the
shops along the piazza.

But the glove shops seemed to have become
branches of Carnaby Street, blasting Beatle records
and *ragas* out of open doorways. The windows were
a jumble of cowboy belts, blouses, shoes, and pants
designed neither for women nor for men, but for some
angular sex in between. Here and there a dress
emerged from the midden, spread-eagled on a panel,
and so short that she surreptitiously yanked hers up
higher.

She walked on to the Via dei Condotti. It was still elegant, but the windows all looked dull, like Fifth Avenue—Gucci pocketbooks, Ferragamo shoes, Rosenthal china, gold Buccellati bracelets studded with turquoise and coral, for some mysterious reason all of it seemed grimly tacky. There was nothing for her here, either.

The stores were closing, too, earlier than she had remembered. All along the narrow street, iron shutters clanked to the sidewalk, and well-groomed matrons with pale lips and embossed eyes rushed by, carrying flimsy little paper bags. What was there to pick up offhand in these supercilious shops? A hand-embroidered bib for a new grandchild, a silk tie, Jordan almonds from Greco's? And where were they going in such a hurry? Not to cook dinner. They had old family retainers for that. Besides, even if they did get home late, who would be there to complain? Roman husbands only came home for lunch. They saved the evening for their mistresses, didn't they?

Robert had not left early enough that day, she remembered. When he got home, he reported the next time they met, the first guests had arrived, and he had been unable to change into a dinner jacket. Jane had been furious, he said. He had been offhand about it, but Molly had detected an edge in his voice.

Blinded suddenly, Molly fled from the shoppers to

the beautiful, littered Bernini fountain in the middle of the piazza. How could she have done such a thing to Jane? How could she have done it to herself, she thought, staring at the flat-smelling water that poured into the stone barque?

The fountain was in shadow, and there was a chill in the air although the evening was muggy. Molly walked back across the piazza, bumped into one of the hurrying women, murmured "Excuse me" without realizing where she was, and bought a copy of the Paris *Times Herald* at the bookstore opposite the fountain. She had probably seen the same news in the *Times* the day before, but reading the paper would give her an excuse to sit on the steps for a while. The sun was still shining there.

Most of the places on the copings were taken by long-haired boys and girls in jeans, but she managed to find a free spot at the level of the house where Keats and Shelley had lived. This trip she would visit it. ("What do you want to bother going there for?" Mike had said when they were in Rome last time.) She picked up the paper. It was the same news. The United Nations was still arguing about the cease-fire in the Israel-Arab war. But page three had some Roman news, led off by an interview with a hairdresser near the Grand Hotel who said he loved Americans. "He speaks good English," said the *Herald*, "and refuses tips since he is the owner." A paragon. She was deep in the classified ads—mostly apartments to let on the Île Saint Louis and *au pair* girls wanted—when she felt a tap on her arm. "Excuse, if you please." A woman with fat, sagging cheeks and gray hair badly dyed blond was thrusting a souvenir map of Rome at her. She put her finger on the Colosseum. "Tell me, please," she said, in accented English, "should I go to the Sound and Light here, or would you advise the Villa d'Este?"

"She recognizes me," Molly thought instantly. "I've joined the club." Or maybe not. Maybe, seeing her reading a paper so casually, the woman thought she belonged here. "You can go to the Colosseum any time," Molly assured her. Clearly she wanted to be told what to do. "This is a perfect night for the Villa d'Este. If you haven't seen the fountains lit up . . ."

The woman folded her map, and sighed heavily. "Thank you, thank you very much. I will go to Tivoli. Thank you." She walked a few steps and then returned. "How do I go?"

Away, thought Molly, just away. "Go up there to the Hassler. Ask the concierge to arrange it for you."

The woman left. Molly looked at her watch and saw it was now time. Leaving the paper, she walked briskly up the steps, down the Via Sistina, and over to the Via Veneto. On the way she looked for a small, pleasant restaurant she knew but nothing was familiar. Then she realized the restaurant she was thinking of wasn't in Rome at all, but in Paris, near the Champs Élysées. No matter. She would find a place later and eat pasta and melon, with no one to complain about what she ordered. "For Christ's sake," Mike used to say, "why do you want to order that? Get something decent." He meant steak. Robert had always ordered for both of them. Whatever he felt like eating himself. Molly disliked meat. She touched neither bone nor gristle, shied away from blood, discarded skin, as though by making the flesh neutral, she could block out remembrance of the living source. (What impressed her about George Bernard Shaw was not *Saint Joan* but his vegetarianism. If *she* had had anything to do with planning his funeral, she certainly would have had him followed to his grave by a herd of grateful cattle.)

She made a circuit of the Via Veneto cafés, half searching for a familiar face, half looking for one empty enough for her not to be wedged between crowded tables nor so deserted that it would be obvious she was sitting alone. She was sick at heart. Was this how she was going to spend the rest of her life? Looking for a place to go between eight and nine o'clock at night? "They eat earlier in New York," she reminded herself. Okay, between six and seven. Once, finding herself unexpectedly alone on Friday night, she had walked down Fifth Avenue after work. The city looked so beautiful in the twilight she could not bear to go uptown to the empty apartment. She walked as far as Thirty-fourth Street, then turned around and walked back. There was no place to go. People were hurrying home, couples were walking arm in arm, cars were racing by. What was there for a woman alone to do in Manhattan on a Friday night between the time offices and department stores closed and theaters opened? It was too late for tea, and she couldn't very

well go into a bar. The double standard still applied:
a man was alone because he wanted to be; a woman
was alone because no one wanted her. She had gone
to Madison Avenue, peered in a Schrafft's window at
the women eating chicken pies, and hailed a taxi.
When she got home, she had opened a can of soup.
"New York should have sidewalk cafés," she remembered thinking then. "We should be civilized, like Paris
or Rome."

Now she settled on a moderately filled café near the
Flora, ordered a Campari, and watched a sad-eyed
peddler make his way from table to table, mutely
winding up mechanical tin toy dogs that no one ever
bought. When he approached her, Molly waved him
away, but he put a little dog down anyhow. Mesmer-
ized, they both watched it gyrate and when it stopped,
Molly thanked him. Then, while she was trying to
decide whether to give him a coin and let him keep the
dog or simply buy the dog and leave it behind, he
packed up his bag and left, leaving her distraught at
having failed him. That was all she ever did, fail people.
She decided to have dinner in a hotel, like a guest on
pension. Cowardly, but it was her first time. Time
enough to brave a restaurant tomorrow. She would go
to the Eliseo roof.

CHAPTER 19

She ordered the *table d'hôte* dinner, complete with Florentine steak and a half bottle of Orvieto, and managed to make the meal last for almost an hour. She sipped the wine, plucked at the rolls, and watched the swallows dip and soar in the darkening sky. It wasn't bad at all, she thought, as the waiter brought the cheese. She was actually enjoying herself. She left feeling so relieved at having gotten through a public meal without taking refuge in a book that she decided to have coffee on the Luna roof.

Only the bartender was there when she arrived. She ordered an espresso, started to say something about the evening, and changed her mind. She was not going to start talking to bartenders and elevator men. Instead she pushed one of the wicker armchairs closer to the railing and looked out at Rome. The swallows were still flying in formation, outlined now against the sky like small, black fighter planes.

She was nearly finished with her coffee when a tall, heavy-set man moved another wicker armchair next to hers. "May I?"

She nodded indifferently. It wasn't her corner.

"Beautiful evening, isn't it?"

She nodded again.

"Your first time in Rome?"

"No," she said, "my third."

"It's my first. Beautiful city."

She nodded.

"I started out taking tours," he said eagerly, "but they don't show you the right things. Like that Etruscan museum. I was walking in the park and I happened on to it. I took three tours and none of them went near it. For my money, it's the best thing in Rome."

"The Villa Giulia?" She was pleased.

"That's it. I had no idea there was so much left of the Etruscans. Some of the stuff looks Greek. Beautiful."

"It's almost my favorite museum."

"Did you ever see anything greater than that married couple propped up with their arms around each other on that big sarcophagus in the middle?"

"You must read *Etruscan Places*," Molly told him, "by D. H. Lawrence. He loved that couple, too."

The man sat back comfortably. "Will you have a brandy?"

"Thank you," she said, "no."

"Oh, come on."

"No, I had a drink before dinner, and wine." She
ought to leave, Molly thought, but she was too tired to
get up.

"Then you want a beer. Best pick-me-up there is."
He snapped his fingers and the bartender hurried over.
"Peroni, two of them, *due*." He turned to Molly. "I
always drink the beer of the country. Tells you a lot
more about the people than the wine. Kirin is pure
Hokusai, with maybe a little of Toyoharu whorehouse
thrown in. Fixx? All the bouquet of a Greek island, a
faint touch of rosemary and olive. Then there's that
foggy, warm stuff they slop up in England . . ."

She laughed aloud. For the first time in weeks. "I'm
Molly Gilbert," she said, holding out her hand, Euro-
pean-style. "Hello."

He took the hand in both of his and shook it gently.
"Ben's the name, Ben Moore. I'm mayor of a little town
in Ohio you never heard of—Hankow, as in China. Nice
town. Mexican beer's misleading, though. Drink a
bottle of Carta Clara and you think the country's okay,
but it's a lousy place, Mexico, lousy."

The beer came. He drained his in one gulp, and
signaled for another. "I guess I'm prejudiced," he conceded. He had a disarming smile. "I just got a divorce
in Juárez. I was going on to Yucatán and then spend a
few weeks fishing at Cozumel, but I couldn't take it.
I hated everything about Mexico. So I figured I better
go someplace else."

They sat in silence for a while. The swallows had

left, and fireflies of light flickered among the dark clumps of trees in the park below.

"Twenty years," he said, "just like that."

She and Mike had been married longer.

"It's not easy," he said, "breaking up a marriage."

"No," she said, "it isn't."

He glanced at her left hand. "You divorced?"

"No."

He seemed disappointed. "You're a widow."

Irritated, she shook her head.

"Then how come . . . ?"

It was none of his business, but as usual, she had to explain. The "tyranny of the shoulds." Questions demanded answers, even when they were not asked. "I wanted to be alone for a while."

"Oh," he said, "you're separated."

The words stunned her. "I suppose I am."

"Any kids?"

"A son." That, at least, was something to hold on to. "He's away at college. Reed."

"One of those longhairs."

"Down to here." She touched the nape of her neck and suddenly longed to hold David close and lean against his vulnerable chest and be safe for a moment. Believe it, she told herself quickly. If David were here now, he would regard her pleasantly from inside his fence and put out a hand to make sure she did not try to open the gate. She had called him before she left, and the moment she tried to tell him why she was going, he interrupted with "It's okay, Mom. No sweat.

You don't have to explain anything to me. Whatever you do is okay with me." He was a good boy. He was afraid she was going to ask him to take sides.

"We don't have any," the Mayor of Hankow was saying. He looked at her appraisingly. "In the beginning, she didn't want children. Then when she did, they wouldn't come, and at the end, it was impossible anyway. She wouldn't sleep with me."

Molly said nothing. It always came down to that, didn't it?

"It disgusted her." He emptied his second goblet of beer and motioned for another. "She hated to be touched, let alone touch. I wasn't even allowed in the same bedroom without I was wearing pajamas. Both parts." He took a deep breath. "I thought it was me. She was the only girl I ever slept with." He stretched. "It's true. She was my high-school sweetheart. Literally. Most warm and loving girl you'd ever want to see until we got married. Then she always acted like she was doing me a favor."

Social work was like teaching, the stigmata showed, Molly thought. Feeling like herself for the first time since she got on the plane at Kennedy, she regarded Ben with professional sympathy and waited.

"I was sure it was me," he confided earnestly. "Then late one afternoon, when everyone else was gone for the day, I don't know what came over me, I walked out of my office to the anteroom where my secretary was typing something up for me, and I stood behind her and put my two hands on her breasts. Didn't say a thing. For a while, she just kept right on typing. Didn't even raise her head. Then her fingers began to miss, she was x-ing things out and starting new lines, and finally she stopped typing and swung around in her chair and faced me." He rubbed his chin thoughtfully. "That was last year. Since then, there's been one after another. Pretty good for a town like Hankow, let me tell you. And now I know for sure. It wasn't me. Not that part, anyhow."

His third beer had arrived. She had barely touched hers. "Cheers," he said.

Molly picked up her pocketbook and moved her chair back. "I have to go. I just got here this afternoon. I can hardly keep my eyes open."

He put his hand on her arm. "Please, just a little while more. Do you want to know something? I've been here four whole days, and you're the first person I've talked to."

She remained seated.

"I don't understand," he said slowly, after a while. "I wanted the divorce, God knows. I had to argue with her to let me get it, and in the end I fixed it so she would have to throw me out. I thought it would be easier for her that way. So why do I feel so lousy?" he asked angrily. "So suspended, with nowhere to go? Like the man in that play by Sartre—you know the one I mean?"

"*No Exit?*" It was the only Sartre play she knew.

"That's it. I saw it on television last winter and I haven't been able to get it out of my head." He closed his eyes for a moment and when he opened them again, Molly saw that they were full of tears. "I'm getting maudlin," he said. "I guess I'm a marrying man."

"Why don't you marry one of your girls?"

"Those tramps?"

He might as well have struck her. Exactly, thought Molly. Deep down that's what they all think, every one of them.

"There's more to marriage than sex," he went on. "If you don't have it, it's no good. But if you do, it's just the beginning. Ironic, isn't it? I walk out because she won't sleep with me and then I can't bring myself to think of marrying one who will. How do you figure that?" He sighed. "I'm sorry. Here I am blubbering about myself, and I haven't let you get a word in edge-wise. Why did you walk out? Your husband start playing the field?"

"Of course not." She was outraged.

"Then it's you." He seemed surprised.

She should go, she thought again, but she still did not move. Instead she rummaged for a new topic and picked up the first one that came to hand. "How did you get to be mayor?"

"I was just kidding. I'm mayor all right but it's a nothing job. Honorary. I run a bank." He signaled to the bartender again. "I'm county chairman, too. Republican. I keep busy. Don't have time to think that way. Forget I'm unhappy. All politicians are unhappy, you know. Don't let anyone tell you different. Happy men don't have to keep winning popularity contests." He leaned forward angrily. "You changed the subject. Why? Did I step on your toes?"

He was incredible, and so was she, to be sitting there.

"If I did, I didn't mean to. It's just that you don't seem to be the type who'd have another guy."

"Why not?" she asked pleasantly.

"Because you seem a cold fish."

"Is that how you get those women in Hankow to go to bed with you?" She was furious.

"No," he said, and his voice was pained. "I really meant it." He shook his head helplessly. "Oh, hell, that's not what I'm trying to say either. I don't mean your looks. What I mean is—you seem more like my wife. A lady. I didn't mean to be insulting. Quite the opposite. Anyhow, I should know better. You never can tell about people, can you? There's this woman I know . . ."

"Forget it," she said, rising finally. "It's okay."

"No, it isn't. I was out of line. I don't know what's the matter with me. I think it's because I'm scared shit-less I made a mistake. I keep going back and trying to figure out where it went wrong and I can't put my finger on it. It's not as though anything snapped all of a sudden. It's more like an elastic band getting pulled and pulled and pulled, and then there's one last pull, nothing special, and the whole thing falls apart. No more give in it. You know what I mean?"

It was exactly the way she had felt during that lunch with Erna. She had thought they had a good marriage, but when she was challenged to examine it, it turned out that its fibers were held together only by habit, like the wrapping on a mummy that disintegrates as soon as it is exposed to the light.

"Yes," Molly told him, "I know exactly what you mean." She started to put down the money to pay for the espresso, anyhow, but he waved her away indignantly. "Thank you," she said. "Good night," and hurried away before he could say anything more.

She walked to the elevator and realized it was the same cage elevator that served her wing. She pushed the button frantically, but Ben had taken care of the check and was standing next to her before the elevator arrived. They went in together.

"Three," she told the elevator operator.

"The same."

"Oh, no," she exclaimed, in a panic. "Please don't do that."

For a moment Ben looked puzzled. "My room is on the third floor. Do you mind?" he said then, coldly.

They rode down in silence. As they got out, Molly said in a small voice, "I'm sorry. I'm truly sorry. I don't know what's the matter with me either." I'm just like you, she thought, scared shitless.

"It's okay," he said. "Forget it. Good night, Molly."

She continued down the corridor, let herself into her room, switched on the light and stumbled toward the bed. Then, still fully clothed, she lay down on her back, put out the light, and stared at the ceiling.

"What am I doing here?" she asked the shadowy surface. What was she doing, lying there in the Roman dark? "The Farmer in the Dell" had come to an end. The cheese stood alone.

She got up wearily, pulled off her clothes without bothering to put on the light again, and crawled back into the damp bed. Could she have stopped at any point? Probably not. What had happened to her was what she had been terrified of all her life. She had gone off the path, just for a second, and now she was lost in the woods.

She buried her head in the unfamiliar pillow, pulled the starched coverlet over her ears and fell asleep instantly.

CHAPTER 20

When she finally woke up in the shut-
tered bedroom, it was with a guilty start, and looking
at her watch, she realized why. It was noon, European
time.

As they had promised, there had been no hammering
on the other side of the airshaft. The room had been as
quiet as a padded cell, there had been not a sound
throughout the long night of her oblivion.

Distressed at the lateness of the hour, Molly gulped
down the stale roll and tea a somewhat dubious room
waiter brought her and dressed quickly. She had
planned to take the subway to Ostia Antica. It wasn't
so much that she wanted to see the excavation as that
the idea of going to a ruin by subway appealed to her.
Ostia turned out to be as touching as all lost cities,

no more and no less—rubble, lizard, poppy, and mosaic all pointing a moral she had no need to learn. Except for a brief lunch at a *trattoria* she was sure Virgil must have frequented, she wandered among the stone streets and crumbled temples all afternoon, courting exhaustion. By the time she got back to the city, all she would have strength for would be to eat in the Luna dining room and go to bed.

But there was a message in her box when she asked the concierge for her key. It was from Ben Moore, inviting her to dinner. She crumpled the note in her hand and tossed it in the wastebasket.

She was in her room only a few minutes when the telephone rang. Ben Moore again. "I've been trying to get you all day," he said. "Don't you ever get tired of walking around?"

She admitted she was weary.

"Are we going to have dinner?"

She should have said she had another engagement, but she was sure he would know she didn't. Instead she repeated that she was too tired to do anything. "Oh, come on," he said, "what are you going to do? Sit in your room on a Saturday night? I'm having drinks right now with a couple from Columbus. Come on down and join us."

Reluctant to hurt his feelings a second time, she agreed to be at the Luna bar in a half hour. The prospect made her uneasy.

"What are you afraid of?" she asked herself with

asperity, as she hung up. "You're a big girl. You're not going off with him, you're just having dinner."

In a way, it was easier having an affair. It was a more familiar relationship. She had never actually gone out with a strange man, Molly realized. When she met Mike, she was only eighteen and he was so young the soft fuzz on his cheeks was just beginning to turn to stubble. He was a friend, and then he was a husband, just as Robert had moved from ally to lover with no hint of strangeness in between. She had never encountered the male unknown. Or had to package herself for approval.

"The most awful thing about being divorced is having to go out on dates again," Eugenia Sachs had told Molly years ago, after her first divorce. (She had apparently survived the trauma because she had been married, divorced, and married again since then. Someone else, Molly couldn't remember who it was, had once joked about how he felt being an "extra" man at a dinner party he went to right after his divorce. "My hands shook so I couldn't tie my tie," he said. "I was nervous as a kid. And then when I got there, my 'date' turned out to have gray hair.")

Ben was nearly bald.

He jumped up, beaming, and hurried toward her as soon as he caught sight of her coming into the small, paneled room. Molly felt better at once. She had forgotten that she did know him after all. The couple with him, however, were strangers—and would remain so, she decided immediately, no matter how many times she might encounter them. She did not like their looks at all. The man had the tall, blond prettiness that Molly, conditioned by Albee and Tennessee Williams, always associated with smiling cruelty; the woman was a cut-down version of the same, a little younger and not quite so pretty, with a hard cameo face and hair that verged on brassiness. She wore a very short, chic, pink-and-white-striped satin tent dress, but her shoes were notably unstylish, jagged-toed and spike-heeled, as if she had decided that she would not allow fashion to interfere with the seductiveness of her ankles. She sat sidewise at the small, round bar table, her legs crossed, and her arches held so taut that her calves bulged.

"Mary Lou Campbell," she announced, as Ben, the politician in him dormant for once, groped to recall her name. She put out a languid hand. Molly was not sure whether she was supposed to shake it or sit in the chair it might be indicating, so she did neither. "Bud Holland. My fiancé." Holland had risen, but as soon as his name was mentioned, he sat down again. After a moment's hesitation, during which she considered how best she might bolt out of the bar, Molly, too, sat down in the chair Ben Moore held out for her.

They turned out to be very sweet. Touching, almost. Ohioans certainly get around, they all agreed. It was Bud and Mary Lou's first time abroad (first time anywhere, probably, Molly surmised). He was en route to Munich for a convention of precision-instrument manufacturers, and they had decided to stop off in

Rome because she wanted to see something of Europe and "wouldn't be caught dead in Paris with De Gaulle, and all."

Her mother was minding her little girl, Mary Lou confided to Molly later, as they walked to a restaurant near the American Embassy Ben had suggested. She was a widow. Her husband had been killed two years before when he missed a turn while riding his motorcycle and crashed into a stone wall.

"The stupid jerk," Mary Lou said wrathfully, "he insisted on buying the damn thing. I begged him not to. I could have killed him when he did it." She had obviously loved him very much. She had been working as Bud's secretary for a year now. They were going to be married by Christmas at the latest. "If not before," she said. "I'm kind of hoping we can make it over Labor Day weekend. Then I could get more time off. But Bud has a lot of things to straighten out." She did not amplify, and Molly did not ask what they were, but Mary Lou did volunteer that Bud had never been married before. Oh, my, Molly thought to herself, but she said nothing.

They had an excellent dinner, Molly happily translating such esoteric terms as *"vitello"* and *"insalata."* It was nearly eleven when they had finished the last sip of the sticky sweet licorice-flavored liqueur their waiter had persuaded Bud to order, and Molly was looking forward to getting back to the Luna, however unexpectedly pleasant the evening had been.

Mary Lou, however, had another idea. "Remember

that place Mr. Sorenson told us about, Bud. With that real low-down show. Let's go there." She turned to Molly. "I've never seen a far-out show. I'm just dying to."

"Strip tease? In Rome?" It was possible, Molly conceded. It was just that she had never connected the two. But then, how would she know?

"Much worse. Really hot," Mary Lou assured her enthusiastically.

"I don't know," Ben Moore put in. For a while now, he had seemed steeped in some private melancholia.

"Oh, come on, don't be a killjoy," Mary Lou chided him. She looked at him curiously. "It's supposed to be a gas."

They left and in the cab, Molly suggested they drop her at the hotel first, she couldn't keep her eyes open, but they wouldn't hear of it, and short of making a scene or jumping out, there wasn't much she could do about it. The address Bud gave seemed to be somewhere in Trastavere, because on the way they passed by the restaurant that had tables in the middle of the street and costumed singing waiters. They turned into a dimly lit street, and the taxi pulled up before a shuttered house. There was no sign of activity. Bud asked, "Here?" dubiously before they got out, and as the driver nodded, making a vaguely obscene gesture, Molly realized she was frightened.

"Do you think we ought to tell him to wait?" she asked, but before she was finished, the taxi had darted away.

A LOVING WIFE

They moved uncertainly toward the house. As they came closer, Molly could hear faint sounds of music coming from the first floor. Bud put his hand out to open the door just as it was flung open, and a blast of sound from a juke box hit them. A cream-colored man with negroid features put his head out and observed them briefly. "Come right in, folks," he said after a moment or two, in barely accented English. "Welcome to our show."

Again fighting an impulse to run, Molly filed into the vestibule after Mary Lou. Ben and Bud followed. There was a stairway directly ahead, but the man barred their way.

"We've got a great show, folks," he said. "Only before you go up, I want to ask the ladies something."

Molly could hear Mary Lou squeal. She herself suppressed a giggle. The entire wall was papered with pictures of nude women, white, Negro, Chinese, fat, thin, small, huge, black-and-white pictures and brashly colored ones. (It seemed to Molly that the colored pictures were mainly of blond white women. They resembled Mary Lou, too, except that Molly didn't imagine Mary Lou's breasts looked quite like that.) With few exceptions, the pictures might have been cut out of *Playboy*, or *Esquire*, or from parking garage calendars. The exceptions apparently were posed snapshots, which Molly found truly remarkable. She had had no idea. Mike's pictures were never like this, she thought foolishly, and then forced herself to listen to the dissertation the cream-colored man was delivering.

"I want the ladies to look at these pictures," he said, still in English, the accent now emerging as not Italian at all, but West Indian or perhaps North African. "Tell me what can be considered obscene about the human body? Is there any greater work of art? Before they go up, I want the ladies to assure me they respect the bodies God gave them."

He flashed his light in Mary Lou's face for a second and, startled, she said: "Oh, sure I do."

"Look at this, ladies," he said next, turning his flashlight up to where the wall met the ceiling in an interesting collage that had been in darkness up to that point. "As Plato, the fifth-century philosopher, said, the love of beauty leads to the Idea of the Good, so the female form is truly divine, right?"

"I don't think . . ." Ben started firmly, but before he could say what it was he didn't think, the cream-colored man had taken both Mary Lou and Molly by an elbow and started them up the staircase. Then he jumped nimbly behind Ben and Bud and herded them up, too.

When they got to the top, they found themselves in a large, bare room with unpainted stucco walls. At the right there was a bar with a mirror festooned with faded artificial roses; at the left, a line of tables surrounded what appeared to be a tiny dance floor. A few nondescript men were hunched over the bar. The tables were empty. As she passed the bar, Molly saw a

A LOVING WIFE

large picture of a Bleeding Heart stuck with arrows taped to one side of the mirror. On the other side, balancing the Bleeding Heart, was a photograph of a sweet-faced young woman in a smock, who stood with one leg resting on a high stool so that her crotch was visible. She apparently had nothing on under the smock.

The cream-colored man settled them at a table and took their drink orders. They agreed whiskey was probably safest, and he relayed the news to the bartender. Then they sat in silence, waiting.

Never, vowed Molly, meanwhile, never again, under any circumstances whatsoever, would she ever go anywhere just for the sake of not staying home. It was a lesson a girl learned the first time she went to a high-school dance with a boy a head shorter than she was. It was a pledge she took on her first blind date with someone who turned out to have wet palms and halitosis. It was something anyone with a grain of sense—or sense of self—knew by instinct. She was a fool to have forgotten it.

After a while, the drinks appeared and a moment or two later, five or six girls came through an archway beyond the head of the stairs. The archway led into a dark, narrow hall which apparently had rooms opening onto it, for trickles of light now seeped through slits at one side of the hall. The girls were very young—fourteen or fifteen, maybe even younger, though their bodies were mature. One was quite black. The rest appeared to be Italian, or Greek, or perhaps Algerian or Moroccan, Molly thought, remembering the cream-colored man's accent. With the exception of the black girl, none of the girls wore anything but white cotton underpants. The Negro girl had a large, unfastened, pink brassière hanging from a shoulder by one strap. The girls sauntered over to the bar, giggled at something the bartender said, got tumblers of what looked like wine or a cola drink, and then clustered around the juke box which was now blaring, "I Wanna Hold Your Hand."

"Holy cow!" said Mary Lou, obviously embarrassed.

"It's a cat house," Ben muttered to Bud.

Bud looked bewildered.

Still giggling, the girls disappeared down the hall again. After another seemingly interminable wait, which could not, however, have been more than five minutes, Molly saw, looking at her watch, their host came to the center of the dance floor. Behind him, a lanky man with a drum settled himself next to the juke box and switched it off.

"Ladies and gentlemens," the cream-colored man said, as the drummer beat a tattoo. "Your attention, please. We are about to start our artistic demonstration. As Plato said in 50 B.C., the Idea of Beauty is the female form divine. Girls?"

No one appeared, and after a moment or two, he repeated: "Girls," in a louder voice, and the drummer beat a second tattoo. Finally seven girls wearing full-skirted, long, black net dresses and nothing else sidled into the room and onto the dance floor.

The drummer flipped on the juke box, and "Ciao, Ciao, Bambino" poured into the room. Faces expressionless, the girls slid past the table where Molly and the others were sitting. They circled and returned, this time with the net skirts over their heads. They were making a third sweep, pelvises undulating lazily this time, when a florid-faced, tough-looking man in dark glasses burst into the room, followed by two perfumed young men dressed identically in skin-tight purple velvet pants and jackets. The tough man flopped down at the table next to where Molly and the others were sitting. The young men took places flanking him, and he threw a heavy arm over each. The older man stank of liquor.

At this point, the drummer began a counterpoint to "Be Seeing You, Baby." The tough man pounded the table with the flat of his hand, and the girls promptly broke into what Molly assumed were bumps and grinds. It was all so matter of fact that it was neither stimulating nor depressing, merely dull. Obviously, this show was only a prelude to their corridor performance, but it was hard to see how the girls could have appeared more disinterested, under the circumstances. They reminded Molly of the girls at Bluebird Cottage. The Negro girl even looked a little like Barbara Jean, *cum* Look. They probably were just like the older girls at Oak Hollow, Molly thought, exposed to everything, ignorant of anything. They never even had orgasms, those girls who sought out gang rape or took on all comers in the backs of cars, Dr. Ziegler always

A LOVING WIFE

said. They felt nothing at all, that was how they managed to emerge unscathed, if pregnant.

Molly sighed. Her hands itched to put slips under those ridiculous net dresses; she lusted for group therapy. Then she became aware of her companions. Mary Lou was looking toward the bar, her face averted from the dance floor and contorted as if she were trying to keep from crying. Bud was staring down at a cigarette he kept jabbing into an ashtray. Ben was standing. "I'm sorry Molly," he was saying softly. "I'm sorry." He put a hand under her elbow. "Let's go."

They hurried down the stairs, colliding in the vestibule with an assorted huddle of men and women who had just turned up unaccountably. Perhaps the play upstairs picked up in a later act, Molly thought, but she couldn't imagine how. Bud, meanwhile, had bolted out of the door and miraculously, seemed to have caught one of the taxis abandoned by the new arrivals before it pulled away.

They were back at the Luna inside of ten minutes. The others were silent during the ride, but Molly, giddy at the reprieve, maintained a running commentary on how interesting the dullness had been, it was hard to see how sex could have been made more stupefying, she supposed the girls turned over their earnings to their mothers and supported their little brothers, while all the while the miasma of the dark-glassed man hung about her, and her eyes saw only the groping of gross hands on sleek purple velvet.

Mary Lou and Bud were staying on the other side of

the hotel—the good side. Ben walked Molly to her room after they left the cage elevator on their side, and for one terrified moment, she thought he was going to walk in with her after he opened the door. But he only handed her the key and touched her palm briefly. "Good night," he said with a deep sigh. "I can't tell you how sorry I am about tonight."

"Don't be," she told him. "It was an adventure."

She undressed quickly and got gratefully between the damp sheets. She felt like kneeling on the floor in thanksgiving that she was back, safe, and then became aware of the turmoil in her body. It was a good thing Ben hadn't come in with her, she thought immediately, bowled over by the realization. Was this what it was going to be like? Was it only her own need that had created Robert, or had he left her with this unrest? Or was this what it was like to be open, and alone?

CHAPTER 21

Sunday was notable for her discovery that it was impossible to find a baby Jesus that did not take after his mother's side of the family solely. Molly was first struck by the identical appearance of Virgin and Child while looking at a Botticelli at the Borghese. Then she pursued her research relentlessly through galleries of Del Sartos, Romanos, Cranachs, Bellinis, Da Vincis, and Titians. She peered at frescoes in Romanesque churches and studied the Raphael rooms at the Vatican. The pictures never varied. The coloring was always the same. Like the Clairol hair-dye advertisements, circa A.D. 1967, they invariably showed medium ash-blond mother with medium ash-blond babe ("Does she or doesn't she? Only her hairdresser knows for sure.").

A LOVING WIFE

It was as fruitful a way as any to spend a Sunday alone in Rome.

She had tried to call Cassandra at home, but there was no answer. When she called Cassandra's office first thing Monday morning, she was told the Signora Savelli would not be in until Wednesday. At least, that was what it sounded like. She left a message saying the Signora Gilbert would like to have lunch with the Signora Savelli when she got back and decided to go somewhere else until then. She could not face another walk to the Spanish Steps, or eat another *café granita* on the Via Veneto. The city was like Pompeii, nothing but dead lava. She decided to get a car and leave it. The driving would present no difficulty. She was used to Italian cars. They had an old Fiat at Quogue. But she was worried about how she could get past the choked streets of Rome when she even had trouble making her way on foot near the hotel. The doorman at the Luna solved her problem. He not only had a cousin who would rent her a car that was brother to the one she had back home, but the cousin lived in the EUR district and would be happy to drive her that far.

It was a fine solution. Hand on horn, the cousin broke through the old city until he reached the wide, ceremonial highway adjoining Mussolini's great white plaster stadium. Then he got out and Molly took over without a tremor. He was a pleasant young man who had grown up in one of the villages to the east where she was heading. He suggested that Molly spend the

night in Scanno, raising his eyes heavenward to indicate
its beauties.

The next two days were like a trip to the moon,
encapsulated, timeless, unfamiliar, healing, taking her
from the full-leafed, fertile Roman countryside to the
proud, bare, bony soil of the Abruzzi, up rugged moun-
tain pass and over narrow dirt road.

She made her way through a flock of sheep to buy a
hand-woven woolen throw from a farmer's wife and
bargained for a copper polenta pot she had no need of
at a stand beside a many-spouted village fountain. At
Aquila, she happened upon a topaz-colored chapel with
a heartbreakingly beautiful rose window and then
found a small tiled inn where she ate pasta which the
owner told her had been cut into strips on the steel-
wired, guitar-like contraption that stood beside the
open hearth nearby. She made a detour to a forgotten
Cistercian abbey mentioned in a footnote in her green
Guide Michelin and encountered a retired postman
from Pittsburgh outside its locked iron gate.

"There's no one here, but I've got a key," he said
eagerly. "I'll take you through."

It turned out the abbey was his vocation. He knew
the carvings on the lintel above the bronze door by
heart and ran his hand lovingly over the medieval
stone of the pulpit. He pointed out the simplicity of
the ninth-century columns and said he intended to
make a spare white candle for the great soaring candle-
stick that stood beside the altar. "I don't know what

A LOVING WIFE

I'd do if I didn't have the abbey to go to," he said. "I'm
kind of lost around here. It's not like home."

He and his wife were living on his pension in the
barren little village nearby, he explained. When they
first came, he told Molly, they "made out all right," but
now prices had risen so they were nearly as strapped
as if they had never lived in the United States at all.

He insisted on taking Molly behind the garden to
see the moss-covered stones of an old Roman aqueduct
he was digging out and gave her a self-deprecating,
wistful smile. "What else is there for me to do? They
don't even have TV here."

She finally managed to break away. Her next stop
was a miniature medieval hill town perched on a crag
so lofty that its view seemed to extend to the Adriatic.
She was feeling her way up cobblestones worn ivory-
smooth by generations of feet and hooves when she
bumped into a couple from Buffalo.

"I was born here," the woman explained when it
became apparent that they were all Americans. "I
haven't been back for forty-seven years."

Molly congratulated her on the charm of her birth-
place.

"I dunno," the woman said uncertainly. She was
forthright and plain, somewhere in her mid-fifties. "It's
not like I remembered. I thought it was bigger. Like
that church . . ." She pointed to a small stone building
with a tiny turret.

"The way she talked about it all these years, you'd

have thought it was Saint Pat's," her husband interrupted jovially.

Molly asked if she had located the house where she had lived.

The woman nodded soberly. "I just come from there." She pointed to a door that could not have led to more than a room or two. Then she looked at Molly sadly, and Molly saw that she was on the verge of tears. "I didn't think the streets were so small," she said.

"Let's face it," her husband told her, "it's a dump." He himself came from Milan, he said. "My relatives couldn't even understand her when she talked to them," he confided to Molly, "they have such a hayseed dialect down here. If you want to see something, take my advice. You go to Milan."

"I like it better here," Molly said.

She did stay overnight in Scanno. The hotel was straight out of Howard Johnson. But when she looked out of her window in the morning, she saw a ravine filled with women wearing striped aprons, long, full gray or black skirts, peasant blouses, and gypsy head scarves. Some were washing clothes in the stream, others chopped firewood on the steep banks. "Is today a holiday?" she asked the desk clerk who had been practicing his English on her the night before. "No," he said. "Why?"

"Because of the native costumes."

"What costumes?"

She explained.

A LOVING WIFE

"Oh, no," he said, "those aren't costumes. That's how the women dress here."

She bought a postcard showing the Scanno women and then didn't know what to do with it. She decided to send it to Barbara Jean. "I am here in Scanno," she wrote, and paused. What else should she say? "Every day I go out and walk but my troubles still torment me"? Should she tell Barbara Jean about her Harpies? She sighed. "Very interesting town," she put down after "Scanno." "Hope you are well by now. Love, Mrs. Gilbert."

She drove through more remote hills, copied an inscription on a monument to a man described as *"prodigo d'opere è d'amore,"* had lunch at an inn calling itself something she translated as "The Lost War," and in the late afternoon came to Chieti. It was an unprepossessing place, suggestive of traveling salesmen and soccer teams, hardly worth even a brief stay, it appeared, but she checked the *Guide* to make sure.

As she had thought, nothing. Just a *villa communale* and a park. The only unusual thing was the guidebook's uncharacteristic burst of rhetoric in its description of the park. It had "acacias, cedars and Judas trees," said the *Michelin*. "In the evening the people of Chieti come here to take the air, and the young people play with their tambourines." Believe it, thought Molly.

She drove through the traffic-laden streets, unfazed now by darting car or pedestrian, until she came to the city's perimeter. Just ahead there was a park area with

224

a large, faded house surrounded by a terrace. She decided to stop and walk around for a while. Obviously, this was the *villa communale*. There were the cedars and acacias. Perhaps those were the Judas trees. It was a pretty scene. A Punch and Judy show was being put on for an audience composed largely of teen-agers, and there was a compact little pavilion where elderly couples and mothers with small children sat eating ice cream. Molly walked over to the puppets; as always, she found them incomprehensible, and was making her way through the park back to her car when suddenly her breath caught in her throat.

Looking past the old house she glimpsed a large, grassy enclosure filled with children. They were holding tambourines, running, tossing, tumbling, turning, and the bells on their tambourines, tinkling, reminded Molly of the sound of goats nibbling cornflowers and thyme in faraway meadows. Every now and then a child laughed aloud, and as she watched, Molly's eyes filled, and something tight in her chest dissolved and melted away.

"'In the evening,'" she repeated to herself incredulously, "'the people of Chieti come here to take the air, and the young people play with their tambourines.' It's the 'Embarkation to Cythera,'" she said softly, "that's exactly what it is."

It reminded her of how she and Mike had felt the afternoon they came upon that young horse prancing on a shimmering hilltop above Delphi.

She turned back to Rome then, racing down the

main highway, and arrived at the Luna not long after dark.

There was no mail waiting for her when she returned, but Cassandra had called. She would pick Molly up at the hotel at one thirty the next day.

CHAPTER 22

Her lids felt so heavy she found it hard to keep her eyes open; she was afraid that if she so much as blinked, she would be unable to pry her lashes apart again. She had three coats of midnight-blue mascara on the lashes, a thick layer of sapphire-blue paste covered her eyelids, there was a faint dab of sky-blue powder under the arch of each of her brows, it was all Cassandra's fault, and she intended to tell her so.

Cassandra had canceled their lunch date at the last minute, asking Molly to meet her in the afternoon instead. Left unexpectedly to her own devices, Molly ended up having her hair done in that place near the Grand she had read about in the *Herald*.

It was not entirely as described. The owner did not

seem to speak English, and he most certainly accepted tips. But he did, as the article had said, have "his own unique way with hair." In addition to Mr. Anthony's usual arsenal, he applied a straight razor, hand dryer and electric comb to concoct a vast Roman beehive out of Molly's short curly hair. "*Magnifica!*" he had exclaimed, kissing his fingers after he twirled the sides. "*Molto bella!*" "Well," said Molly, peering into the mirror, "I suppose." Then she added politely: "*Grazie.*"

It wasn't that the style was unbecoming; it just appeared superimposed, like a wig. When she went to the front to pay, the woman at the cash register (who wore her hair pulled straight back in a knot, Molly noted) looked at her and shook her head disapprovingly. "Too bad," she commented, in English (perhaps, after all, *she* was the owner) and Molly's heart sank. "Such a beautiful coiffure," the woman continued, "and the face, so naked. How can you go out in the street like that?"

"I could wear a mask," Molly replied humbly, and the woman laughed. "I mean," she said, "don't you have your eye *maquillage* with you?"

"Never use the stuff," Molly said, and the woman blanched.

"*Prego*," she said, "we will put a little something on the eyes for you. No charge," she added hurriedly. "Our pleasure," and before Molly could protest, she murmured in Italian to a young woman sitting idly at a manicurist's table nearby. Her eyes were rimmed with kohl like an ancient Egyptian's.

The girl got up, hurried Molly into a nearby booth and, without consulting her, began to dab at her eyelids. When she was finished, she handed Molly a hand mirror, and smiled proudly. What she saw stunned Molly. She looked as if she had stepped out of a Fellini movie—like a dissolute *contessa* from *La Dolce Vita* or *8½*. She tipped the girl and returned to the woman at the cash register. *"Bene,"* the woman said, nodding in approval. "Very good. Now the *signora* looks like herself."

Molly should have gone back to the Luna and washed it off but she couldn't resist seeing the expression on Cassandra's face when she first caught sight of her. That whole year Cassandra was at the Center doing her fieldwork, she had teased Molly about her spare make-up and the "mouse" colors she wore to the office. "If only you had more eyelashes, and a red dress. You could look like Audrey Hepburn if you just tried a little," she had said. "Only not so skinny," she added, upon reflection.

"You're crazy," Molly told her, cherishing the comparison. "Anyhow, you're wrong. She wears beige and gray, too."

Summer or winter, Cassandra had worn chunky jewelry, high heels, and bright prints which clung to her body like wet jersey. She had been a joy to behold, Molly remembered, and even more of a joy to work with. In theory, she had been Cassandra's supervisor, but she had learned as much from her as she had taught. It would be good to see Cassandra again, she thought, warmed by the prospect.

She turned into the Via Barberini and looked for the building where Cassandra's agency had its office. They were to meet in the café on the ground floor. It was a little early, but Molly went inside anyhow. Cassandra always arrived ahead of time for an appointment. She hated to keep anyone waiting. (She used to keep her wristwatch five or ten minutes fast, and until she caught on to why they were doing it, they all used to make a point of asking Cassandra the time, for the sheer pleasure of seeing the flash of alarm with which she contemplated the subtraction and translation involved in her reply—her otherwise perfect English failed her when it came to numbers.)

But the café was empty except for a middle-aged man and a pencil-slim, tall, young girl wearing a sleeveless satin shirt open nearly to her navel. They were sitting close together in a booth near the door, looking at each other with such unabashed passion that Molly averted her eyes as she walked by them to a back table.

Five minutes passed, then ten. Molly became worried. This was unlike Cassandra. She had just decided to go upstairs and see if something else had happened to delay her when Cassandra walked in. Molly's first reaction was amusement. Cassandra's eyes were as made up as hers, only she had used brown shadow and for some reason she had the stuff underneath as well, so that she seemed to have pouches. Then as Cassandra, smiling, came closer, Molly realized that she wore little, if any, make-up. Her eyes were simply dark with fatigue.

"I should have taken it off," Molly said at once, "but I thought I'd surprise you. Anyhow, you're responsible." She felt like a fool.

"I like it," said Cassandra staunchly after Molly explained. "The blue matches that Pucci print you're wearing." She had on a gray cotton suit with a white blouse. She looked very thin. "It's good to see you, Molly," she said. "You look wonderful."

Molly mumbled something.

"I'm sorry I'm late. I had to take a long-distance call just as I was leaving." Yes, she said, she would like a drink. Vermouth, please. "Where have you been? I've been trying to get hold of you for two days."

Molly explained.

"But why the Abruzzi?" She was clearly puzzled.

"Well," said Molly, "it's near. I didn't want to drive too far by myself."

"Oh," said Cassandra, "Mike isn't with you. I was wondering why he didn't join us."

"He couldn't get away," said Molly.

"I spent the war in Scanno, you know. That's where my father was exiled. I must have told you."

Dr. Franceschi had been one of Italy's leading historians, Molly recalled, and a firm opponent of Mussolini. "I didn't realize it was Scanno," she said.

"Oh, yes. That's where my mother sent me to keep house for him. He must have been living alone for a

couple of years before that. I went to the Scanno school,
too, only I couldn't learn anything. The teacher used
the dialect. I couldn't understand a word she said."
She smiled ruefully. "That made us even. No one could
understand me either. The class used to laugh every
time I opened my mouth."

"It must have been terrible for you—especially at
that age," Molly said sympathetically, and she told her
about the woman from Buffalo, and how her Milanese
in-laws had scoffed at her Abruzzi accent. "She said she
just stopped talking Italian after a while," Molly said.

"Oh, it wasn't that bad. I had a good time after
school. I liked Scanno."

"I'll tell you the place I liked," said Molly. "Chieti.
It's not far from Scanno."

"Oh, yes, I know it." Again Cassandra looked at her
curiously. "Why in the world would you like Chieti?
It's such an ugly city."

"Not really. It seemed idyllic to me."

"Idyllic? Chieti?"

She told her about the Judas trees and the acacias
and the children playing with their tambourines.

"What's so special about children playing with tambourines? Every child plays with tambourines."

Now Molly looked at her.

"It's a ball game. A little like badminton, I guess.
They come in sets. Tambourines and balls both, little
balls, big balls, rubber ones, plastic. I just bought a set
for my nephew for his birthday."

"Oh," said Molly, crushed, mourning for Chieti and

the colt that had escaped over the hill at Delphi. She could have wept. "Nothing is the way it seems, is it?" She noticed that Cassandra had drained her vermouth like water. "Do you want another one?"

"Why not?" Cassandra made a small pile out of the damp paper coasters the waiter had put under their glasses. "Is there a conference in Rome I don't know about?"

Molly shook her head.

"Oh." She seemed relieved. "A pleasure trip."

They could go on exchanging platitudes from here to the Tiber, Molly thought. It must be her eyes. They were putting Cassandra off. Making her feel hostile. "No," she said, taking a deep breath, "not a pleasure trip." She could not stop looking at the couple in the front booth. He wore a wedding ring although, obviously, he was not married to her. They were kissing avidly now. How could they be so open about it, and so cheap? She turned to Cassandra. After all, she lived in Rome. Three thousand miles from anyone they knew. Far enough away to make telling her all right. Besides, it was not fair to sit there like a fatted calf, swathed in Pucci, exuding security. It was not fair to either of them.

She told Cassandra why she had fled to Rome. "I sound like Ben Moore," she berated herself. "It's all this liquor on an empty stomach. I should have had lunch," but it had been such a long time since she had spoken to anyone, she could not help herself. Or maybe it wasn't the liquor. Maybe it was just speaking English.

In the past, paradoxically, she had felt more at ease in a strange country when she did not speak the language. You were clearly a tourist, not an outsider, as you were in London, say, if you didn't know anyone—but it hadn't been working out that way this trip. For days now, talking pidgin Italian, she had felt like a half-wit. It was a relief to be able to talk freely. She could not stop talking. It was as though Robert had died. As long as she talked about him, he was alive again.

"I'm not sorry," she told Cassandra. "I'd be lying if I said so. It was overwhelming, the most complete experience I ever had. I loved the way he looked. We laughed at the same things." She forced her eyes away from the couple in the booth and looked at the door instead. Let him turn up, she prayed, let him just step through that door, dear God, and I'll do anything You say. "The thing is," she continued calmly, "where do I go from here?"

"Why go anywhere?" Cassandra asked.

"I can't keep running."

"Stand still."

She was being obtuse, but how could she be expected to understand? Then Molly noticed that Cassandra's mouth was quivering. Instinctively she put out her hand just as Cassandra reached for it, and they clung to each other.

"That call I had to take," Cassandra said, "was from Perugia. I thought I had it all arranged for someone to come—that's why I couldn't meet you for lunch. I had to stay and work it out. But I have to go back there anyway tomorrow."

That explained it. "Giancarlo's still there?"

Cassandra nodded. "It's almost two years now. A long time. I go up every weekend. If I have to, more often." She gave a little laugh. "As you see. But he's still better off there. He likes the country, he's very good with his mother's tenants, they look up to him. He's even talking about getting the vineyards in shape again."

Giancarlo was about ten years older than Cassandra. He came from a vaguely noble Florentine family. His mother and Cassandra's had been friends all their lives, Molly knew, and Cassandra used to say she had been in love with him as long as she could remember. He had married someone else first though. That was probably why Cassandra had decided to come to the United States. It was the same year. When her mother wrote her that the marriage had been annulled, Cassandra went right back. Less than a month later, she wrote a blissful letter saying she and Giancarlo were married. It was really a marvelously romantic story, Molly thought, except for one detail. No one had thought to tell Cassandra that Giancarlo was an alcoholic.

"It's a long trip to make every weekend, isn't it?"

"Not bad. No more than to Long Island. Besides, I have a car now." Her face lit up. "Remember my Vespa? I still miss it. I was so free riding it, like a bird . . . so much better than a car!" She threw up her hands. "A car's so bourgeois."

A LOVING WIFE

"Do you still go home for lunch?" At least she would be driving if she did, Molly thought. The last time they saw her, Cassandra had said she couldn't go out with them because Giancarlo wouldn't eat unless she was there. She used to roar home on her motor scooter to have lunch with Giancarlo (assuming he could be persuaded to have any food) every single day and then come back to the Via Barberini. With all the traffic, it took her nearly an hour each way. Contemplating Cassandra's life, Molly had been torn between exasperation and inordinate admiration. Some envy, too. Even then she had envied Cassandra's total dedication to Giancarlo. (She was like Erna, Molly realized now. What was there about Italian men anyhow?)

"Not if I can avoid it. To tell the truth, one meal a day with my parents is enough."

"You're living with them?"

"Where else?" Cassandra shrugged. "My mother is too old to manage alone. Unaccustomed, I should say. And with the maid situation what it is . . ." She closed the subject abruptly. "It's funny," she mused, "I used to look at you and Mike and think that was what a marriage should be. You seemed so suited to each other, two against the world, shoulder to shoulder always."

Molly had a quick flash of the contented couple demonstrating their devotion through eternity on top of Ben Moore's Etruscan sarcophagus. "We were," she said. "I always thought we were. A pair of prototypes. A good husband. A loving wife." She winced, and closed her eyes for a moment. "It's not Mike's fault," she told Cassandra after a while. "He didn't do anything. Nothing he could help anyhow. It's me."

Cassandra nodded.

"I can't stand myself."

"Who can?"

Molly shook her head. "Oh, no. You have no idea what I mean." Then she asked her the question she had always wanted to ask. "Didn't you ever think of leaving Giancarlo? Getting a divorce?"

Cassandra looked her full in the face. "Every day. What do you think?"

She was just saying it to make her feel better, Molly thought.

"But it's not possible in Italy, and even if I could, I wouldn't. What for? What is, is. Nothing changes. I gave up expecting anything to change long ago."

How old was Cassandra now? Thirty-four? Thirty-five? Not much more. "You shouldn't feel that way," Molly said. "You're much too young. It's different with me. It's only going to get worse for me from now on. Not," she added, "that I can make myself believe it. I keep thinking it's all a mistake. I'm going to wake up, and everything will be all right. This is just temporary." She looked sheepish. "I sound like a client, don't I?"

"A little," Cassandra agreed. "I wish I could fool myself, but I can't." She sighed. "You don't know how good it is to be talking to someone. Not that I don't have anyone to talk to, but . . ."

"I'm going back to New York."

"Exactly." She laughed and then went on soberly. "I

A LOVING WIFE

couldn't stand it at first when I realized what I got myself into. You know how impatient I am. I screamed, I yelled, I was a regular Magnani. Oh yes I was," she insisted, seeing Molly's gesture of protest. "I wasn't going to accept it. Not me. I tried everything. Giancarlo, too. Don't think it's the way he wants it. He tried. Analysis, a clinic in Geneva—he even took a mistress. Part of therapy, he assured me. Nothing helps. I think he was born with something missing. Or maybe it's his mother. Who knows? Whatever it is, I have to live with it."

"How?" Molly tried to think of what it was that she and Mike had quarreled about, but she could not.

"I'll tell you how. I keep myself in a strait jacket. That's what I decided when I saw nothing would help. I made up my mind not to expect anything—no home, no children, no entertaining, no nothing. That way I wouldn't keep on being disappointed. I wouldn't struggle against it, and so I wouldn't get hurt. Sometimes," she said, her voice catching, "I feel that I have shrunk so that even a strait jacket is too big for me, but . . ." She could not go on.

"There isn't a strait jacket made that could contain you," Molly said, deeply moved, greatly ashamed. Seeing herself through those deep-welled, brown, exhausted eyes, she seemed contemptible—selfish, spoiled, immature. It wasn't fair. Of all people, Cassandra, who should have had a houseful of children and a husband who would cherish her. "I can't bear your being so alone," she added.

"Oh, I have a friend." Cassandra seemed a trifle amused at Molly's intensity. "That's part of the strait jacket. We meet Thursdays usually. First the hairdresser, then Paul. It's a routine. Like tooth brushing."

"You really feel that way?"

"I think so." She considered Molly for a moment. "You see, the only one I really want is Giancarlo. That's my sickness. Because he doesn't want me. Ever. Or any other woman, for that matter. He has other tastes."

"My God," said Molly. "That, too?"

"That, too. Anyhow, my friend isn't free either, and if he ever was, the first person he would drop would be me. Besides, Giancarlo would kill me if I ever left him for someone else. Don't look so surprised, Molly. It's true. He's a very frightened man, and frightened men are cruel, you know that."

I'm a fish out of water, Molly thought—a big, gasping fish flopping along dusty hotel corridors. I don't understand anything, or anyone, any more.

"Life isn't pretty," said Cassandra. "You've always been so sheltered, so—so optimistic . . ."

"Don't give me that unsophisticated American bit," Molly interrupted, suddenly angry at Cassandra, at herself, at the whole world.

"Oh, no," Cassandra assured her, "it's not American at all. You're like my mother. Trusting. Essentially helpless. It's very charming."

"Me? Helpless?"

"Weren't you just telling me how awful it is to be alone?"

"Well, yes," she conceded, "but that's not because I'm helpless. I'm just surprised to find how much I mind it. I thought I'd like it." She realized something. "You had your own apartment when you were in New York. You seemed to like it. Did you?"

"I adored it."

"Maybe it's because I've never been alone in my life —except for that short time during the war."

"It's different when you've never been married," Cassandra said, "when you're young. You want to be free then, I guess," she went on slowly. "I guess that's the real reason I went to live with my parents when Giancarlo left—for myself, not for them. I'm lost not having to be responsible to anyone, not having to take care of anyone, even if it's only from Monday to Friday."

"That's what I mean," said Molly. "And it seems to work both ways. For me, anyhow. I'm not only used to taking care of people, I expect to be taken care of." She had never been aware of it before. "You're right. I am helpless in a lot of ways. I've been spoiled all these years. Why, I've never even been anywhere by myself before. I never drove so much in one stretch. Mike always does the driving; I just spell him." She stopped to think about it. "Actually," she continued, "again, except for the war, and that doesn't count, everyone was in the same boat, I've never been without a man to run interference for me—first my father, then

Mike. I've never had to take care of luggage, or make a reservation, or tip anyone, except a waiter or a doorman calling me a taxi. I've never even had to choose a restaurant except to have lunch near the office."

"It's almost the same for me," said Cassandra, "except for that trip to America."

"And we're emancipated," Molly reminded her. "Career women."

"You know, I don't even like to sleep alone," Cassandra said. "Not that way," she added hurriedly. "I mean just alone. It never bothered me before. But after Giancarlo left—before I moved in with my parents—I used to put a chair under the doorknob. For protection."

"It's like being able to read as late as you please. Now that I can, I don't. I sleep so fitfully I'm exhausted once I go to bed. Then there's eating," Molly said eagerly. "I used to love to eat alone when Mike was out. But the thought of actually having to cook for myself, or eating alone in a restaurant . . ."

"Awful," Cassandra agreed. She glanced at her watch and Molly could see her lips moving slightly. "It's getting late," she said, and seeing Molly's grin, her eyes crinkled. "Do you think there's any significance, doctor, in my always wanting to push time ahead?" She reached for her purse. "I have to go. My mother always waits for me to fix supper. They'll be starving. Why don't you come home with me? I picked up some marvelous *tortelini* this afternoon."

"Thanks, but I don't think so. I have some things I have to do. I'll eat later on at the hotel."

"I really wish you'd come," Cassandra persisted, but she was clearly relieved.

It was time for them to part. They had ventured too far as it was. There was a layer below which people should not go together lest they find themselves strangers when they return to the surface again. It was not at all true that everyone was alike underneath. Deep down, deep deep down, we live in a buried Tower of Babel, intelligible only to ourselves. If that. "Another time," said Molly.

As they walked out, Molly noticed that the front booth was empty. She must have taken her eyes off the lovers, after all, since she had not noticed them leave. Surprisingly, it was still light enough outside for their eyes to have to adjust after the murkiness of the café.

"I'll drive you back to the hotel," Cassandra offered.

Molly said she preferred to walk. "But I'll go with you to the car."

They walked in silence to the little piazza where Cassandra had parked and when they got there, Cassandra said softly, "It's not really a strait jacket. Forget I ever said it. I was just feeling sorry for myself."

"I know. What's true today is different tomorrow." But not for her, Molly thought to herself. She's lying, and she knows it.

Cassandra kissed her good-bye. "Another thing. Just

because a door is open, that doesn't mean you have to walk through it."

"I know that, too."

Cassandra got into the car, leaned over and turned down the window. "If you do decide to go to Spoleto for the concert this weekend, call me. Maybe you can come and stay with us at Perugia afterwards."

"I will," Molly promised. Then she put her head through the open window. "Cassandra," she said, "take care."

By the time she got to the Via Veneto, her feet hurt, but she did not go back to the hotel. She could not bear the thought of going into that wretched room just then. Instead she sat down at the first free sidewalk table she saw and shamelessly ordered a Coca-Cola. With peanuts. She needed them after the three vermouths.

She sat there through the twilight and into the night. Figures passed back and forth in front of her as if they were on a moving sidewalk, but she barely noticed them. Once a young man with long sideburns and a tightly fitted embroidered coat sidled up to her and said, "May I?" but she waved him away absently. After a while, she noticed the waiter nearby and, guilty at having occupied the table for so long, she got up and went down the street to Doney's, where she ordered a lemon ice. She had decided not to have dinner either. At the far side of the street the man with the toy dogs was working his way along the tables. She also thought she recognized Ben Moore sitting with a man and a woman, not Mary Lou and Bud Holland, new people.

He had his back to her, but she could see that he was gesticulating exuberantly. He had probably been drinking too much. She discarded any fleeting thought she might have had of going over to say hello.

Instead she sat staring into space. Finally, out of the corner of her eye, she saw the man with the toy dogs wind up a dog at the table next to hers. He waited until it ran down, then, unaccountably, packed up his valise and walked away without approaching her table. Curious. It wasn't possible that he remembered her, was it?

At that point, she rose quickly. Molly in night town, she thought. Lost among the lost. She would end up as a painted tin dog, jogging on unfamiliar tables, wooing strangers who didn't even know she existed. Besides, her eyes itched. It was time to go upstairs and wash her face.

When she got up to her room, she studied her watch. A little before eleven. That meant it was about five in New York. She picked up the telephone, wondering whether there was still service at that hour, and by a miracle, the switchboard answered. She asked to be connected with the overseas operator. Important decisions should be made on the spur of the moment—wasn't that what her father always said? Or was it Sigmund Freud? Sometimes she got the two mixed up.

He was not at the lab, and there was no answer at the apartment. It was unlikely that he would be there but she asked the operator to try the Quogue number anyhow. It was Thursday. He might have decided to take a long weekend.

The telephone at Quogue was picked up on the first ring. She heard a woman's voice say "hello" and the Rome operator identifying herself before she was cut off. When the operator came back on, she asked Molly whether she should leave a message for Quogue to call, her party was expected back soon. "No," Molly told her, "never mind leaving your number, just cancel the call."

Who could it be? He couldn't have found anyone that fast. Not in such a short time. He wasn't the type. Anyhow she was too tired to care. Had no right to care. Didn't care, she assured herself. It had been just a notion. She settled herself into bed gingerly. For some reason every muscle in her body ached as if she had the flu.

Maybe Kate had dropped in. She had a key. It didn't sound like her voice, though. What had probably happened was just what she should have expected. He had found someone. It never failed. There was nothing unpredictable about life. You just had to figure out the likeliest irony. This one was routine. If she had seen it once, she had seen it a dozen times. Wives walked out, and husbands remarried. Simple.

Feeling oddly relieved (Nemesis had finally dropped the shoe), she read until one, then switched off the light.

The buzz of the telephone awakened her. As she picked up the receiver, she glanced at the watch on the bedside table next to the telephone. It was seven o'clock.

"Hello." Yes, this was Mrs. Gilbert. One in the morning in New York, then.

He was connected. "Hello. Hello, Molly?"

"Yes."

"I got the message that you called. Hello," he repeated when she made no comment, "you there? Are you okay, Molly?"

"Yes," she said, "I'm okay."

"I waited to call until now. I didn't want to wake you up in the middle of the night."

That was nice of him, she thought. She said nothing.

"What's up?"

"Well," she began, and took a deep breath. She had done wrong, no use trying to weasel out of it, and that was that. She had behaved badly. But she didn't have to keep on throwing herself under the train to prove how sorry she was. Enough was enough. It was time she started to forgive herself. If she didn't, who would? "Mike," she said brightly, "I called because I had an idea. Why don't you come over? We could go to Sicily. You've always wanted to go to Sicily."

There was silence at the other end.

Apparently she had awakened with a headache. Her head was splitting. She tried to form the word "please," but she couldn't get it out.

"I can't," Mike said finally. "It's impossible for me to get away right now."

"All right." She was ready to hang up. "It was just an idea."

"I tell you what," he said then, "why don't you come home now and I'll take some time at the end of the summer. Maybe we can get away then."

Now she was confused. "I can't, Mike," she said, speaking naturally for the first time since the telephone woke her. "I'm on one of those fourteen- to twenty-one-day deals, remember? I have to stay at least another week. Otherwise I have to pay the regular fare."

"Pay the two dollars, Molly," he said. He also sounded like himself for the first time.

"Well," she began, dubiously, but before she could say anything else, he said shortly: "It's up to you, do what you like. This is an overseas call, you know. I'd better be going. 'Bye, Molly," and hung up.

She stared at the dead receiver for a moment, then put it down, shattered. She lay back on the bed and thought for a while, then got up. It *was* up to her. Besides, what was two dollars, compared to what she had spent already?

She got on the telephone again and by eight thirty, she was at the airline terminal in Rome, ticketed for a ten-o'clock flight. At the airport, rushing to board, she was informed her plane was not leaving for another two hours.

"The aircraft was late taking off from Kennedy," the clerk at the counter explained. "Lots of congestion there these days." He looked at her reflectively for a moment and then said: "I'll be glad to send a cable for you if anyone is meeting you."

She started to shake her head, then changed her mind. No reason why she couldn't let him know she was coming back. Especially if it didn't cost anything. She gave the clerk the name and address.

❀

The plane took off at exactly high noon, and she had the day flight she had always wanted. It was much better than flying by night, just as she had thought it would be.

They arrived on time. When she walked into Customs, she looked up at the balcony of the International Arrivals Building and routinely scanned the faces. For one stunning moment, seeing a tall, dark figure at one side, her heart stopped for a second, but it was only a visual trick. When she looked more closely, the man did not resemble Robert in the least. Mike was nowhere to be seen.

She opened her suitcase for the Customs inspector; told him her declaration was correct, she had bought only one pot; closed it, summoned the porter, and walked into the lobby. Mike was standing just outside the doors, a small bunch of climbing roses wrapped in aluminum foil in his hand.

"Hi," he called, coming over to her. "How was the trip?"

"Fine. Very smooth."

He handed her the flowers. "Here. I thought you'd like these. First of the season."

She looked at him, unbelieving.

"You're always saying how nice it is the way people meet each other with flowers when we go to Europe," he explained, obviously terribly embarrassed.

"They're beautiful." She could feel her eyes welling up.

"I thought we'd go back to Quogue," he said. "I've been out there since Wednesday. I asked the Burkes out, but it's all right, they went over to Easthampton this morning." He looked at her questioningly. "I hate being alone."

"So do I," she told him. "So do I." She hesitated. "Mike," she said, feeling desperate, "I'm sorry."

"For what?" He put an arm around her, pulled her to him briefly and then released her. She could feel him shaking when he held her. His face looked drawn, and he had lost weight. "I'm sorry, too," he said. "I try, but I guess . . ."

"It was my fault."

"Water under the bridge." He moved toward the exit, and she followed him, looking back every now and then for the porter. When they came to the outside doors, Mike stopped. "Where's your bag?" He put a finger under her chin and turned her face toward him. "I saw a cartoon the other day," he said. "It shows a couple sitting in their living room and she's looking up from a book and asking him whether it was 1958 or 1959 that was the winter of their discontent."

Molly made no response.

"You had to be there to appreciate it," he said resignedly. "Anyhow, let's say 1967 was our winter, and let it go at that, okay?"

She nodded. Then she saw the porter. "There he is, Mike."

Mike gave him a dollar and took the bag from him. "I'll go for the car," he said. "I tell you what. Why don't you call your mother in the meanwhile? I talked to her a couple of times this week. She's worried about you."

Molly telephoned her mother and told her she was at the airport.

"Good," said her mother, "I won't keep you. As long as you're back safe."

When she hung up, she thought of calling David in Seattle but she couldn't think of what she would say to him if she got him. Tell him that she had turned up again? She found herself beginning to dial Oak Hollow, and decided against that, too. What was the point of talking to Barbara Jean just then? Except to take her mind off the business at hand.

It was a good thing she had two weeks more, she told herself. She was going to need them.

Taking a deep breath, Molly walked outside and waited for Mike to drive up. She didn't know whether to watch for the Buick or the Fiat. He must have gone out to the beach in the Buick, but he loved to drive the Fiat.

She looked around her. The weather was beautiful.

Warmer even than Rome. He was wrong, she told herself, it hadn't been winter, it was glorious summer, and it would never come again.

Now she saw Mike edging toward the curb. He had come to the airport in the Fiat, just as she had thought.

She walked to the car. Maybe it would be better if she only stayed another day or two. They could use the time she had left to do something together in the fall.